THE OUTSIDERS

Edited by Joe Mynhardt

Proofread by:
Joshua Hood and Nancy Scuri

Crystal Lake Publishing
www.CrystalLakePub.com

TABLE OF CONTENTS

WELCOME TO PRIORY

KEVIN LUCIA

CLOSE-KNIT COMMUNITIES offer its members many wonderful things. Much needed support in a time of crisis. A sense of family. A sense of belonging to something greater. An intimacy often lost in the crowded hustle and bustle of city life. In a community, everyone knows you and your parents, your triumphs and failures, and a community is eager to celebrate the former and console the latter. A community exists for the good of its people and stands ready and waiting to meet their needs.

But consider, for a moment, a community founded by a man driven by an iron resolve and a dedication to Something Older. A man who indeed serves a greater vision, something powerful . . . and Other. Imagine a community—perfect in appearance, desirable to those outside it—committed not necessarily to serving the needs of its people, but rather serving the needs of that Other. A community connected and bound by their service to a Nameless and strange being demanding absolute conformity and obedience.

Welcome to Priory. A gated community that everyone wants to get into, but the price of admission is high, as an unbalanced bigot discovers in James Everington's "Impossible Colors." Priory is forever, and though a person may leave for a time to experience life outside its walls, Priory's voice always calls back its own, sooner or later, as we see in Rosanne Rabinowitz's "Meat, Motion and Light."

Priory is a place of deep religious fervor (fanaticism?) in which the only thing more important than family and community is the Thing That Lies Below its smooth streets and picturesque homes. Service and Faith in Priory supersedes everything, even grief over the loss of a child and the desire to be free of that grief, such as in Stephan Bacon's "Stolen From The Sea."

In the center of Priory in a mansion lives Charles Erich, the man who runs Priory, the mouthpiece and spokesperson (and high priest?) of That Which Lies at the Heart of this wonderful community. But Charles Erich is a man of unknowable secrets, of things not meant for the average man. The kind of secrets than can shatter the mind as quickly as it does a marriage, as seen in "Precious Things," by V.H. Leslie

Even those outside Priory's walls aren't entirely safe. Police officer Michala Bruce discovers the hazards of examining Priory too closely in Everington's "Impossible Colors," and of course, people living in Priory do work in the surrounding area of Exham, and attending a business party inside the walls of Priory carries a greater risk than mere social embarrassment in Gary Fry's "The Subprime."

The Priory. A community of one mind and

purpose. A place of order, commitment, peace, and service. A perfect world, building on mind shattering secrets from beyond the pale. Enter . . . if you dare.

THE SUBPRIME

GARY FRY

LEE WAS WATCHING raindrops roll slowly down his windscreen when he decided to make the call. It had been pouring down all morning, and his car—a BMW coupé, credit-funded by his new job—was soaking wet. After dialling, he recalled his childhood—his warring parents, his desperation to be free of them—and the habit he'd developed when nervous. The drops of water, with their erratic movement and eerie silence, had always calmed him.

But then his boss answered the call.

"Hi there, Lee. What can I do for you?"

Lee mustn't assign telepathic powers to the wily middle-aged man; he'd obviously just seen his employee's name—Lee Mann—on his mobile phone screen.

"Oh, hi, Mr Philips," Lee replied, hoping the nervousness in his voice would be ascribed to the poor connection. He was sitting outside in the company car park, but the weather must be affecting reception. His boss would be in his office, seated at his vast desk like

"

some imperious king. "I just wanted a word with you about my job."

"You're a good man, Lee. I've been impressed by your first year in post. You've made some fine killings. I don't offer *everyone* my direct contact number, you know."

All of which made what Lee had to add more difficult. Mr Philips had been good to him, offering a role selling mortgages after only one interview. The older guy claimed to have an eye for talent, could smell people's ambition. Lee certainly possessed that (even though much of it was driven by fear, a refusal to return to poverty), but maybe what Mr Philips had failed to identify was his conscience. The simple truth was that Lee didn't like doing to people what the job entailed.

He first tried spinning it another way, saying the hours he worked interfered with his social life and that he had plans for further education. But Mr Philips smelled the lies slipping from him, like fish stains on the fingertips.

"Listen, lad, I know how you feel. I go through this with almost every new recruit to the business. It's just a touch of cold feet, you know. You're young, you're beginning to nail down aspects of your identity, and you want to be a good person in every sense. I can understand that. Hell, I went through just the same at your time of life."

Mr Philips hesitated, presumably to let Lee absorb this string of reflexive insights, which, in the absence of a decent father, had considerable impact, a persuasiveness that went with the territory in the housing game. Lee watched more raindrops stream down the glass, one joining others in a small river that accelerated. This put him in mind of the Philips Finance sales team, the way he'd initially felt as if, with many other young colleagues, he was part of a family. But that was before he'd been asked to violate principles that surely characterised any worthy communal unit. He'd grown up with enough involuntary corruption; he hadn't expected to *choose* it later in life.

Just as Lee was about to issue a floundering response, his boss went on.

"Look, I don't know where you are at the moment—out with a client or on the road—but why don't you hurry back here for a face-to-face chat, eh? We'll open a bottle of something, talk it through. What do you say?"

Even though Lee was unable to see the man's office window from where he was parked at the building's rear, he had the sudden impression that Mr Philips could see him, that his eyes were everywhere in the property, like the CCTV cameras maintained for security. Irascible customers, feeling ripped off, had been known to travel miles to deal directly with their concerns. But it wasn't as if the company did anything *illegal*. The police had always been called, and they weren't required to deal with moral dubiousness.

Feeling compromised in his resolution, yet returning some of the good faith Mr Philips had offered, Lee agreed to the impromptu meeting. He said he'd arrive in about half-an-hour—time enough, he hoped, to get his reasons for leaving fixed in his mind.

As he hung up, more raindrops continued falling down his sodden windscreen, joining identikit comrades in a pattern that resembled a network of savage cracks.

He'd decided to quit his job with the company alone last night in his flat. His income—quite a generous sum for a 19 year-old, fresh off welfare support—had allowed him to pay the bond and rent of a plush city-based pad on a canal-side. These were old factories renovated by investors, a glossy sheen added to their essential character. Lee had always been interested in property, maybe because he'd never lived anywhere permanent in the past. The council estate on which he'd grown up had always felt tenuous, like a plot of land claimed by Gypsies.

After leaving home the first chance he'd had at 16, he'd spent much of his time out of work boning up on effective ways of making money. Finance was the sector that had appealed most, promising cars, girls and status. Despite his studious nature, he wasn't *that* different from other young men of his generation. And when he'd seen a job advertised selling subprime mortgages, he'd applied immediately and, following a cocky display at interview, had been offered the post.

Months had passed, during which he'd learned much about the mortgage business, drawing on garrulous confidence and an intuitive understanding of human psychology. He could, as the saying went, "sell sand to Arabs," but as the job unfolded and he was asked to work in other areas of business activity—the company also bought property at hefty market discounts—he'd begun feeling uncomfortable.

The truth was that he wasn't happy implementing certain practices established by Philips Finance. One involved offering a fair price for the property of people who—for a variety of reasons, often pitiable—needed to sell quickly. The company promised an uncomplicated purchase, but bogus delays were introduced, maximising client desperation, until, close to completion day, the price was reduced for other mendacious reasons: a last-minute check identifying high crime rates in the area, for instance. Few customers went ahead with the sale, but enough did to make these sneaky methods worthwhile. It didn't cost Philips Finance a penny to play with people's lives in this way.

But what was it doing to Lee's character? This was the question he'd asked himself in bed the previous evening, his stomach churning after hearing that a client he'd recently outfoxed with a 40% property discount had burned down the house in protest . . . with his wife and children inside. Nobody had died once the fire brigade did its sterling work, and the company could reclaim the investment sum through insurance, but Lee had felt guilty anyway. Then he'd decided to take his skill-set and burgeoning knowledge into worthier ventures, maybe retraining in another financial sector. Ever cautious, he'd put enough money aside to fund a college course and, now determined to progress in this way, would chalk up his time at Philips Finance to experience.

Provided, of course, that its owner allowed him to do so.

As Lee approached the man's office, nodding to his dutiful P.A. (whom he'd been meaning for a while to ask out on a date), he sensed his heart rate running at a wild canter. And after entering the room at the front of the building, which overlooked the whole city, he was reminded why he always felt so ill at ease in his boss's company.

Mr Philips oozed self-assurance to an unusual degree. A long-term survivor of constant duress, Lee thought he knew a thing or two about people, but he'd never come across anyone so single-mindedly bullish and determined as the middle-aged man. While visualising his boss in his mind, Lee always imagined an imperiously aloof sea creature—a shark, perhaps, which was fitting because the man kept a plaque on his desk bearing some kind of nautical beast. But this one was very different from any fish-like species. It more closely resembled an octopus, bearing great suckered tentacles with opaque probes at their ends . . .

But he was supposed to be handling his resignation.

Mr Philips had already greeted him, poured him a drink, and sat him at his desk; this had all occurred in a hyper-efficient blur, as if the guy had just cross-tabulated time and profit in a mental chart and decided to complete the task as soon as possible. Lee shouldn't feel offended; he was just a useful cog in an expanding machine.

"Now listen, son, I'm going to do something today I've rarely done in the past for relatively new recruits to my enterprise. But you're a good man, have shown great promise, and I think you're worthy of such investment."

"Er, well, thank you, sir. But-"

"Hey, look, just hear me out, okay?"

The interruption having served its intended purpose, preventing Lee from saying more, Mr Philips paused to draw breath. The man was slender, with a gaunt face, as if he practised restraint in all other aspects of his life except business. Looking ineffectually on, Lee wondered where the man lived, what his family was like (he wore a ring on his third-left finger, some kind of gold sailor's knot), and what he did during recreational periods. Might he belong to a close community, or maybe even a church; that would surely account for his placid demeanour, as if he drew strength from a spiritual source of well-being.

Then the man went on.

"Here's what I propose. I just got off the phone to my wife at home and she's in agreement with me. This weekend we're planning a dinner party, just a few friends and neighbours. And we'd both be delighted—as, I'm sure, would our guests—if you'd agree to come along, too."

Despite his decision to quit and move on, Lee couldn't help feeling flattered by this invitation. Only a few years ago, he'd lived in a bedsit with a bunch of other no-hopers, with only a few stolen textbooks for stimulation. And now here he was, on the cusp of being introduced to the backbone of England, to the fiscal weight and social *mores* of the middle-class. Success had no moral considerations; you either made it or you didn't. The devil was always in the detail, but if the print concerning that was small enough, who the hell cared? Lee certainly didn't agree with these sentiments, but nonetheless understood them; it was how the world worked, and who but fools cut against *that* grain?

Nevertheless, deep-rooted decency forced him to say, "That's very kind of you, sir. And I hope you'll thank your wife, too. But the truth is that I came here to offer my resig-"

"To continue offering your frankly sterling abilities to the company. *That's* why you came here, son, and that's why I'm so appreciative. I believe turnover during the last year, since you started, has almost doubled. That's down to a number of initiatives I recently set in motion, but I personally consider *your* recruitment a significant factor. I'd certainly hate to lose you now. We're on the brink of achieving such great things, son."

Lee's eye returned to that illustrated plaque on the desk—the octopus-like entity with such hideous suckers. It looked like it brandished complex probes, each conducting experimental activities on whatever it chanced upon underwater . . . But Lee's mind had wandered again; he needed to deal with this situation.

"May I ask if, in the future, there are plans for the company to avoid some of its more . . . dubious ventures?" he asked, his voice trembling a little in the older man's presence, but his innate confidence carrying him through. "You see, *that's* what's been troubling me. I'm sorry, but I just can't set aside my feelings for the sake of business at any cost."

"Why not?"

The brevity of the question surprised Lee, knocking him off his expected course. "Well, I . . . uh, I don't know, really." He thought quickly, one hand gripping his glass—the whisky his boss had poured, possibly to ease persuasiveness. Refusing to drink, Lee added, "My conscience, maybe?"

"So you believe that *I* lack a conscience?"

"Ah, no, I'm not necessarily saying *that*. But—"

"Logic would suggest it, I fear."

Again the man's bullish comportment, the unshaken way he stared across the desk with eyes as green as some tropical sea, threatened to defeat Lee. Usually so smart with his mouth, Lee was now bereft of anything to say. The truth was that he'd inadvertently offended his boss, in such a way that to backtrack would undermine his whole rationale for resignation. He believed this could be described as "caught between the devil and the deep blue sea", and as Mr Philips continued gazing his way, Lee believed the phrase had never been more apt.

But then, mercifully, the older man relented, his severe expression diminishing as he spoke again, this time less forcefully.

"Please, just come to dinner in a few days. I simply want to show you that doing what we must do to earn a good living is not incompatible with leading a good life."

What did this mean? What activities would Mr Philips describe as a "good life"? Lee had to admit to being intrigued to discover; despite working for the man for about a year, he'd never got beyond the enigmatic front he presented. He wasn't sure *anyone* in the company had, even though he'd discussed the issue on several occasions with colleagues.

Intuiting risk, possibly even danger, Lee gazed back at his boss, whose eyes now looked even greener—as green as the water surrounding that octopus on the plaque. But Lee refused to look again at that and then made a final comment.

"Okay, I'll come. But be aware that it'll take something significant to make me change my mind."

Mr Philips grinned, not a common expression in Lee's experience; his teeth looked as sharp as blades. "Oh, I think we can manage that," he said, and then yielded up his home address.

Staff came and went at Philips Finance; during his time at the company, Lee had seen at least six people join and another six leave. Most were young men like him, eager to make the leap from dismaying anonymity to city-based player, to living life in the fast lane and satisfying all their testosterone-fuelled desires. He had no idea what had become of those who'd struggled to handle pressures of the work, but imagined some had dropped out to seek less demanding jobs. He certainly hadn't heard from any of them again.

One reason could be because he'd never been much of a friend-maker. He suspected that wariness arising from his rough youth had compromised his ability to form casual relationships. He wasn't one for women, either, but often found them greatly attractive. He didn't think he'd ever invite Mr Philips's P.A. for dinner, not if he was leaving, but there'd certainly be other candidates for a future Mrs Mann. He was only 19 years old, after all.

He steered his Beemer according to directions issued by a foxy lady on his satnav unit. His boss had offered a full address, printed on a calling card quite unrelated to the business. This boasted another illustration of the freakish sea creature, but Lee had paid little attention to that, instead programming the windscreen-mounted device and simply driving. It was Saturday evening, and while a million other young guys were out on the town and the pull, he was headed to an older man's pad, to meet him and his wife and their friends and neighbours. He hoped it wouldn't be *too* dull; he was no party animal, but if the folk he was about to meet looked likely to proselytise on behalf of an unorthodox communal lifestyle, they'd certainly picked the wrong dude to convert.

As Lee neared the place indicated by the satnav, he reflected again on impressions about his implacable boss. The man was calmness personified, a rock of stability in the tempestuous sea of the current UK housing market. Did such self-control come with age and experience? Lee doubted that over-simplistic explanation; after all, his dad remained as foolish today as he'd ever been, an aggressive hedonist with all the ignorance of his social class and then some. Lee hadn't spoken to the man in years, and although he called his mum from time to time, there was little love lost between them. He'd gone one way while they'd remained stationary. Fuck em.

Lee was bright and self-aware enough to realise that this hole in his private life had left him vulnerable to another family—the Philips clan, perhaps—filling the void. He'd already considered the fact that his boss had become a father-figure, offering an opportunity when everyone else had seemed to sidestep him. But this had come at a cost, as such things always did, and despite his best efforts for a year, it was a price Lee was unwilling to pay anymore. He supposed he'd agreed to this dinner invitation for old time's sake; he owed Mr Philips at least a chance to persuade him not to leave.

At last he'd reached his destination. Priory, a few miles outside a fine town called Exham, proved to be a gated community, which didn't surprise Lee at all. He'd known the man would live somewhere rarefied and exclusive. What was surprising, however, was the level of security in operation here. Despite the moonlit October murk, his headlamps picked out a huge white wall which appeared to ring the small community and was crowned by a mass of electric wiring, barbed and coiled.

The locality—affluent, leafy, clean—hadn't looked like the kind of place that bred vermin similar to people he'd grown up with. This made Lee wonder why those living here were security conscious to the point of hurting potential intruders. Again a flash of danger arose in his mind, but after spotting a large gated entrance—perhaps the only way into the place—he pushed aside such fearful nonsense. He'd come to attend a dinner party and not an evening of black magic rituals.

Although a small booth was stationed to the right of the gate, nobody was presently inside it. Maybe the place was patrolled by a physical presence only at certain times of the year. There must be a camera controlling entry, however, because as soon as he drew near in his BMW, the gate started sliding slowly to one side. Airport car parks, Lee recalled from his only holiday abroad (a trip to Spain alone earlier this year), had automated systems that recognised number-plates, but there was no reason to assume such sophisticated technology here. The gate was probably triggered by electric pads under the driveway's tarmac; it would remain active during sensible hours, and lapse into snooze-mode overnight, when residents were unlikely to receive visitors.

At any rate, Lee was soon able to enter Priory, leaving all hopes behind as the gate—a steel unit, whose wrought iron sections displayed another rendition of that curious sea creature from his boss's desk—slid slowly shut in his wake.

The community consisted of a circular arrangement of streets, with one long single lane leading across an imaginary diameter and flanked by rows of nigh on identical housing. These were one storey properties, most with voluminous, well-tended gardens, and garages for vehicles positioned at the end of short driveways. Streetlights combined with the uncertain moonlight rendered each building luminous, as if they all possessed a spectral grace matching their detached nature to an unsettling degree. The housing looked simultaneously inclusive and aloof, communal and misanthropic.

Looking down the street directly ahead, he spotted a noticeably larger property at the heart of all the residential streets—this boasted gothic turrets and arched windows—but Lee recalled that the house to which he was headed was number twelve. After turning right to cruise slowly along one of the curving streets on the estate's outer circumference, he examined posts at the foot of each driveway. Here was six . . . eight . . . ten . . . And that was when he chanced upon his destination, a smart looking building with a single light burning above the front doorway. The light was red. In other circumstances, Lee might have found this alarming, but now he merely shoved back such intrusive thoughts, parked up in front of the house, and climbed out of his coupé.

The property's garden path divided a neat stretch of lawn bordered by hedges and only a few highly regimented plants and flowers. Advancing for the front door, Lee wondered why a man pulling in about £100,000 a year was content to live in such a modest dwelling. The building was certainly nice—compact and tidy—but Mr Philips could surely afford more. But maybe that was the point about this community; regardless of how they earned a living, perhaps residents had forsaken consumerist concerns, preferring to exist in non-competitive ways. The soul had greater needs than ego-enhancement—hadn't Lee once heard his boss say this, during some inspirational meeting speech?

Just then, he noticed the grass to each side of the path was sodden. He slowed, placed one Gucci toe on the lawn and heard it squelch, water oozing between countless blades. But this made little sense. How could the grass be so wet and the path remain dry? If the lawn had been watered earlier, wouldn't a hosepipe have also rendered the stone dark and freckled? Lee wondered whether the gardens here had some kind of under-floor maintenance mechanism, a suspicion heightened when he heard something groan beneath him, as if great plumbing pipes ran this way and were presently summoned into action. But then the impression faded and he switched his attention back to his goal.

After knocking at the door, he turned to examine the street again; Its uniform housing and sparse vegetation did little to settle his anxiety. Maybe he was troubled by the absence of people hereabouts and lacked anything to focus his thoughts upon; there weren't even of the usual furtive curtain-twitchers at work this evening, as there usually was whenever an unrecognised car arrived in such an otherwise silent residential area. Only a few other vehicles were parked alongside the kerbs or up driveways, each sensible saloons or family hatchbacks. If Lee ever had to describe a stereotypical middle-class suburban scene, this would be it.

At that moment, as Lee was most disarmingly distracted, he heard the door open behind him. He turned at once, having now realised that the knocker he'd used earlier boasted another rendition of the tentacle-burdened beast from his boss's desk and calling card, this one moulded from brass. But now someone else claimed his attention: Mr Philips was standing over the threshold, smiling in an effusive way Lee had never witnessed before.

"So glad you could make it, son," said the man, holding out one hand for a shake. He was dressed in a loose shirt and casual trousers, a real contrast to the sharp suit Lee had elected to wear. In truth, Lee had expected something grander, more formal, but as he was led inside the property—the hallway was painted and papered in a simple, restrained style—it appeared that the evening was likely to be more homely, even family oriented. Coupled with his boss's use of the personal term "son", Lee began to feel uncomfortably compromised.

After being directed into a lounge (similarly decorated, with solid if unremarkable furniture), he was introduced to a surprisingly large number of people. One couple, almost certainly in their 30s, had come from next-door, while an older pair occupied the house opposite. Ostensibly a single man lived on the nearest corner, and a similarly unattached woman was based two doors down and worked in the local community centre, supporting voluntary initiatives for those less fortunate than themselves. There was only one child present, a pleasant, dark-skinned girl who beamed up at Lee as he gave a brief wave; she was maybe eight or nine, and the two adults accompanying her—who couldn't be her parents, as both were white—seemed the least stuffy members of the gathering.

Once Mr Philips returned from another room with a drink for the new guest, Lee suspected that this event had a purpose other than mere socialising. This was evident in the way people held their bodies, a kind of expectant, simmering quality he associated with important meetings, where deals could be offered or withheld. Even when Mrs Philips eventually appeared from what must be the kitchen, Lee's impression failed to dissipate. For one thing, there was no small talk among the guests; for another, no light music was playing, which left the silence between utterances almost pregnant with unease.

But then Lee's boss, having dealt with standard formalities—freshening up drinks, introducing Lee to his quite attractive, mumsy wife—summoned the group to attention in his usual self-assured way.

"I'd like to thank you all for making the effort to attend our little soiree. In addition to our friends and neighbours, we have another guest this evening. Allow me to introduce Lee Mann, one of the ablest members of staff I've employed in all my years in business. But as is often the case—we'll all remember, of course, being in this situation before—Lee has more recently questioned his involvement in my organisation, to such a degree that, alas, he's thinking of moving on. You're correct in assuming that this is, again, a *moral* issue, but I'm assured that we all know what must be done."

Lee wasn't sure he cared for this introductory monologue; watching the man standing in one corner of his pleasant lounge, he observed all the others in his peripheral vision, finding them no less edgy in comportment, as if about to tackle "what must be done." And what *was* that? Lee would surely discover by listening to more from his boss.

"Priory is a respectable place. Yes, it draws on income from a variety of necessary and not always honourable enterprises, but it's what we do with such money that counts. We enjoy one of the most peaceful and co-supportive communities you'll ever encounter. Our streets are clean, our older residents cared for, and our children educated and well-fed. We as adults are healthy and altruistic. There have been no documented examples of psychological distress since the place's inauguration. For all this, we must thank Charles Erich."

This name, its bold syllables, put Lee in mind of a Nazi war criminal or maybe the leader of some notorious cult, long since sent to prison for the good of the world. In the sudden silence left by Mr Philips's paused narrative, Lee imagined he heard more of that underground plumbing at work, a splash and gurgle of activity rendered sonorous by depth. But then he felt compelled to speak.

"Who is Charles Erich?" He paused to look around the group, observing eleven people gazing back, all their eyes greenish in the lounge's low light. "Is he here tonight?"

"Mr Erich is our unofficial leader, the architect of Priory." This came from Mrs Philips, the first time she'd spoken other than issuing a hearty hello after Lee had arrived. Despite being married to such a distinguished man, her face looked reverential while discussing this eminent other. "He's responsible for the maintenance of property and upkeep of the place's infrastructure, but he likes to keep a relatively low profile. He's certainly no social animal."

So what other kind of animal is he? Suppressing the sinister nature of his latest thought, Lee decided that Charles Erich must live in that ghostly building at the head of the street, the one he'd spotted at a distance bathed in frosty moonlight. It had been a creepy place; Lee actually felt relieved that the community leader wouldn't join them tonight.

"This is all really interesting. I'm pleased you all live in such a great place," said Lee, striving to keep unrest out of his voice. Then he made the point lying at the heart of his concerns. "But despite feeling flattered that you've asked me here, I'm not really sure *why.*"

His boss started walking towards him, his grin undiminished. From the corners of his eyes, Lee saw the other residents close in slightly, as if deliberately reducing the space in which he had to manoeuvre. But surely this was anxiety-induced paranoia. As another of those subterranean sounds struck up, Mr Philips placed one arm around Lee's shoulders and started guiding him elsewhere, to what resembled a dining room through an open doorway beside the kitchen, from which fine aromas now filled the house. Then his host spoke again.

"We simply want to show you that the way we earn a necessary living has nothing to do with the way we live."

"Hi, I'm Ben Weston, a stockbroker. This is my wife, Penny, who works in insurance."

"I'm Linda Simpson, an estate agent."

"And I'm Luke, her lesser half; I'm in accounting."

"The name's Kevin Johnson. I've worked in agency recruitment all my life."

"Mary Jeffries, a retired solicitor."

"And what do you guys do?" Lee asked from his position at the centre of a lengthy dining table, around which all eleven other diners were now seated, enjoying a starter Mrs Philips had just delivered, a rich pâté with fruity relish. After spontaneous introductions more informative than the brief ones Lee had been offered upon arrival, he'd directed his question at the couple with the child, seated three-in-a-row opposite him.

"Nice to meet you. I'm Harry Links, a business studies academic. My wife can speak for herself."

"For all my sins, I'm in banking. Lana's the name. And this fine young lady is-"

"Claudia," said the dark-skinned girl sitting between these two adults and now grinning toothlessly. "I'm eight and live with my mum, but she's away at work right now, so Mr and Mrs Links are looking after me."

Christ, thought Lee, looking at the girl with unwitting intensity. *She's only 11 years younger than me. How things change in just over a decade, the innocence in large, moist eyes replaced by cynical exasperation . . .*

Lee mustn't forget what he he'd planned next week, quitting work at the homeowner's company. If all this—being treated to a fine meal and initiated into the Philips' cherished community—was intended as some kind of emotional bribery, he'd have to resist at all costs.

But that didn't mean he had to be rude. Smiling at all the guests, who'd just freely engaged with him, he said, "I'm very pleased to make your acquaintance." Then he turned to his hosts, both of whom continued eating just as the rest did. "This is a delicious pâté, Mrs Philips. Did *you* make it?"

"She prepares all our meals," Mr Philips snapped back, using one hand to briefly stroke his wife's back. "We're all very self-sufficient at Priory. We minimise outside influence whenever possible."

Lee understood the impulse—it was a helluva world, what with burglary and vandalism—but he was again struck by its obvious hypocrisy. All the residents had jobs in highly profitable sectors—estate agency, insurance, banking, the legal system, and more—and he'd bet his final pound that each had their snout in troughs as muck-filled as those in which his own enterprise scavenged. It was how things were, which was not objectionable *per se*, but coupled with such a grand claim about communal rectitude, it was pretty hard to take.

Nevertheless, Lee said nothing and continued eating his starter, washing down each fine mouthful with a glass of red wine which had been served by his hospitable boss. Indeed, Lee's lingering unease had led him to sup a lot from a bottle, his glass topped up at regular intervals until he felt quite fresh. He must be careful; he'd be driving home later. He certainly didn't want to put himself at risk of an accident.

The large amount of liquid he'd consumed—more latterly, to ease reception of a dull conversation about business between the Weston and Simpsons—made him eager to use the toilet once plates from the first course had been cleared away. He took the opportunity presented by a brief silence to ask Mr Philips where the bathroom was, and the man greeted his request with another smile, the widest he'd worn all evening.

"It's just along the corridor, through that door." He pointed at a second opening, opposite the one by which they'd entered. "Take your time. The main attraction awaits you upon your return."

He meant the second course, whatever his wife now prepared in the unseen kitchen. This smelt rich and pungent, but Lee was unable to identify the scent. He'd believe it to be fish if not for a meaty undercurrent, like chicken basted in some concentrated sauce. In any case, he soon stood and moved for the exit, observing eleven pairs of eyes following him all the way. His impression that his companions were now preparing themselves for some final assault was immediately disowned, dispatched the same way the contents of his empty wine glass had been. Then he was in the hallway his boss had mentioned, thankful of a period of merciful solitude.

There was a picture on the wall next to the bathroom entrance; it displayed another sketch, in faded pastels, of that gargantuan sea creature, the one Lee had spotted on his boss's desk and on the property's front door knocker. Lee thought he might have even dreamt about this beast the previous night, dramatising details only hinted-at in these depictions: the bulbous head and multiple eyes, the invasively long tentacles, the organic instruments it used to fillet food. Did the thing lie at the bottom of oceans, snatching up passing prey, before demolishing them with intricate haste? The monster in *this* drawing appeared to have extracted the spine of some other sizeable tenant of such dark green waters; it clearly meant to devour the leftover meat.

Maybe this was why the image had violated Lee's psyche. Having read some business psychology, he knew a little about Freudian theories and how deep concerns were translated into approximated imagery, helping the mind process them during sleep. Perhaps the creature represented Philips Finance and the process of deboning was a subconscious acknowledgment that, by quitting his job, Lee might lack backbone.

Or maybe such paranoiac speculation was just bullshit.

Lee looked away from the picture and then forced himself to ignore a new impression, one involving a kind of chanting nearby, maybe even back in the dining room from which he'd just fled. Surely he only imagined this; the words, muttered in the rhythms of a chant and perhaps even a religious one, sounded like no language he'd heard before—in fact, he couldn't be certain it actually *was* language. The vowels seemed misplaced, the consonants clustered meaninglessly together, many a "Cthl" and "Fht" and "Nyar."

Shaking his head, he quickly entered the bathroom, which was as unspectacularly stylish as the rest of the property. He dropped his fly to urinate while thinking about what was happening this evening, what the residents of Priory were trying to achieve. Did they have a specific routine planned for later, or was the goal to simply let him absorb their decency, their honourably modest existence, by osmosis? Was he supposed to go away with the realisation that, despite the necessarily messy things he was expected to do in the workplace, this didn't preclude the pursuit of a good life? Mr Philips had pretty much suggested as much after inviting him over. But right now, the plan's implementation seemed a little vague to Lee.

He zipped up and then flipped on the sink's hot tap to wash his hands. As water trickled down the plughole, he thought he heard another of those deep, booming noises, as if something vast was stirring underneath the property. Perhaps the community was powered by standalone generators and even a bespoke plumbing system. If Charles Erich, the absent "architect", had designed this place with independence in mind, that wouldn't be surprising . . . Lee shut off the tap, hoping the subterranean sounds would soon cease.

But they didn't.

Rather than being mechanical, these noises now sounded organic, as if something wet and heavy was slinking around just below the floor of this tidy house. He sensed water splashing nearby, maybe in the sink unit's pipes, but more likely beyond the toilet's u-bend. This was more than the standard flush Lee had activated a moment ago, and which had settled since. It resembled one thing, or perhaps several, darting through liquid, wriggling and lashing, while slapping with rubbery resonance against the hollow material of the bathroom suite. Lee wanted to believe that the sounds were moving away, but the unsettling truth was that they seemed to be getting closer to him.

He quickly turned away and exited the bathroom, just as something in his wake seemed to break a surface of water. Lee heard liquid trickling, as if running down the sides of a lengthy object poking up through a rippling tide. Had a probe, like those at the ends of the tentacles of the illustrated monster he quickly passed again, just emerged from the toilet bowl?

But that was absurd—laughable, even. Indeed, Lee immediately pushed aside the thought, making his way back into the dining room and sitting at the table which, in his only brief absence, had greatly changed.

The first thing he noticed was the crockery. Very different from the small china plates on which the pâté starter had been served, these larger ones appeared to have been crafted from some kind of ivory or maybe fragments of bone. The surface of his own was rough, but he suspected it was deliberately so; polishing would rob the substance of its essential character, its pale colour and even delicate scent.

He had no more opportunity to examine the plate before spotting his glass standing behind it. This had been topped up, but not by more of the red wine he'd consumed earlier; the new liquid was *green*, rather like the seawater he'd seen in that hallway sketch . . . But no, *stop* that, he instructed himself. Then he quickly glanced around and realised that everyone else had a serving of the same drink; some had already made a start on it, surely indicating how harmless it was. Anxiety mobilising him, he reached forwards and snatched up the crystal glass, drawing it to his lips and then sipping.

The stuff tasted good, like a heady combination of mint and liquor. Lee wondered whether this brew was another Priory production; the residents seemed big on that. The drink was certainly alcoholic; as soon as Lee swallowed, the toxic ingredients started feeling for his mind the way a sea monster tracks prey . . .

But again he suppressed such nonsense, looking quickly up, just as Mrs Philips—the only person previously absent—returned carrying a huge silver salver. Potatoes and vegetables (locally sourced, maybe?) were already steaming in bowls at the middle of the table, and soon his host's wife had placed the main attraction there, too. Then she lifted the heavy lid.

"What is it, Mr Links?" asked Claudia, her dark-skinned, eight year-old face looking eager and expectant as she gazed up at one of her two guardians.

"It's what Barbara has kindly prepared for us all," Harry Links replied, his expression devout as more of that rich aroma Lee had detected earlier—a simultaneously meaty and fishy scent—suffused the room.

At least Lee now knew the woman's name. Her husband—Lee's boss—was called Harvey. Barbara and Harvey. They sounded about as threatening as some amiable couple in an old TV sitcom. So why, as Barbara fished meat from her grand serving tray, did Lee now feel decidedly unsettled?

The food that emerged was hard to identify at a single glance. It appeared to be lean chunks of something, but whether it was land-based or sea-life, it was impossible to decide. Steam stretched away from it, like tangible limbs, coiling and twining, before dissipating in the space above the table, where only a single lamp burned with a greenish tinge. The uncertain light, coupled with Lee's mounting unease, prevented any further analysis until, plate by bony plate, the cook dished out the evening's repast.

"So tell me, Lee," said Lana Links, once everyone had started loading up with supplements to their main foodstuff, potatoes and vegetables aplenty, "how did you come to work with Harvey?"

By this time, Lee had taken another few sips from his green drink and was feeling quite tipsy. Mixing alcoholic beverages had never worked for him, possibly a psychological effect caused by recollections of how his dad had behaved after sinking pints and chasers in the pub every other night. But he wasn't about to divulge all *that* corrosive material; he'd be appropriately vague in reply.

"I drifted around for a while, I guess, exploring potential opportunities. Then, when I saw the post advertised, I just went for it. The work seemed appealing. I've always been interested in property."

He hadn't wanted to talk about his job; it seemed risky, somehow, as if all the Philips's friends and neighbours might try to persuade him to remain with the company.

But then Linda Simpson, an estate agent (if Lee remembered correctly; booze now swirled his thoughts around), said, "And quite right, too. Nothing is more important than our homes, is it?"

"What about long-term financial security?" asked Ben Weston, and at once Lee recalled that he was a stockbroker.

"In the event of unfortunate incidents, insurance is crucial, too," added Penny Weston, thumping the tub for her profession, the way all the others now seemed to be doing.

Indeed, moments later, Kevin Johnson, in the recruitment game, said, "Everything, of course, relies on maintaining regular employment," and that was when Lee realised what the gathering was up to.

The nice house, the pleasant social event, talk earlier about desirable communal relations, and now all these practical considerations for a secure life . . . The Philips' must have briefed their guests prior to the meal about the doubts Lee had experienced lately, asking them to make a show of respectability and play up all the virtues of gainful employment. It was an amiable conspiracy, but at least his understanding precluded more unsettling thoughts about underground creatures and any physical danger in which he might have placed himself. The monster in the picture must be just some stylised avatar representing Priory, maybe even an idiosyncrasy of the eccentrically aloof Charles Erich. At any rate, it had nothing to do with Lee and he should cease thinking otherwise.

After hacking one end off the portion of meat on his plate, he brought it to his mouth and started chewing. Although the substance smelt fishy—a sharp, pungent odour—it tasted more like chicken marinated in strong spices: cinnamon, perhaps, or maybe paprika. It had a lively, aromatic aftertaste which even more sips from his fresh drink did little to temper.

By now, the whole room had begun squirming and blearing, but Lee, his inhibitions loosened by alcohol and possibly even feeling a bit defensive, was nonetheless able to contribute to the conversation.

"There are many aspects of the job I like," he said, finally swallowing a first mouthful of the weird fish-meat hybrid. Then he drew breath, thought for a moment, and simply said it. "But I'm afraid there are others I'm not so fond of."

"It's a helluva world at the moment, fella," said Harry Links, the business studies academic who'd no doubt possess all the answers about markets and the economy. "We all have to do what we have to do to get by."

"Yes, but," replied Lee, his confidence increasing

after all the booze he'd consumed and having finally elbowed his way into the discussion, "but there are certain activities involved in the role that I . . . well, that I consider unnecessary and even unethical."

"I find it hard to believe that Harvey would expect you to do anything *illegal*," said Mary Jeffries, whom Lee recalled was a retired solicitor and now a voluntary worker for noble causes.

"The regulators would put a stop to that in the financial game," added Luke Simpson, whose accountancy was presumably as spotless as the way he dressed, in plain, smart clothing just like all the other guests' garments.

By this stage, woozy engagement had sunk Lee into trouble; the tenderness of the meat and all the drink swimming under his tingling scalp combined to leave him vulnerable to further comments. Then he glanced across at his host, at imperious Mr Philips, who simply sat grinning widely, as if it was now his turn to speak.

And that was when he did.

"What formal qualifications do you have, Lee?"

Feeling as if the room had just got smaller, Lee put down his knife and fork—they made a dull sound against the strange ivory-like substance of his plate— and looked again at his boss.

"You know as well as I do that I have none," he replied, the shame that might attend such an admission becoming pride about his success anyway. "You employed me on the basis of a hunch about my abilities—a hunch I know that you consider accurate."

If he was now feeling cocky, it was probably self-righteous independence speaking. He'd overcome far more threatening people in the past than this bunch of communal-minded neighbours, with their self-justifying hypocrisy. Recalling his father's fists, which he'd once regularly fended off, he went quickly on.

"I'm a good man, and good in every sense. I'm afraid this evening has made no difference to my belief in that." He took another mouthful of the meat, drank more from his glass. He realised he should be grateful for these offerings, but no longer saw them as anything other than transparent bribes, petty deal-sweeteners he witnessed far too often in his profession. He considered himself more sophisticated than the company's average client; he certainly wouldn't be bought. "I'll be resigning first thing Monday morning."

"And go where?" asked Mr Philips.

"I'll . . . I'll worry about that later," Lee replied.

"With no formal reference?"

"If that's the way you want to play, so be it."

Just then, another rumble besieged the property, as if whatever lay beneath had grown disgruntled, a fitting reflection of the homeowner's clearly mounting frustration. Or *was* Mr Philips displeased by these latest developments? After all, the man's smile never faded. Would he wear such an expression if he was displeased? Lee seriously doubted that; he had much experience of the man. The only other time he'd seen him express such pleasure was after securing one major deal or another.

And what achievement could be as sweet to him here?

"You're *subprime*, Lee," said the proprietor of Philips Finance, and that was when that underground noise became fiercer. If Lee had earlier thought it resembled a creature moving way below, it now seemed much closer, as if it had gradually ascended and surveyed everything happening in this deceptively innocuous room. Then, with venom, his boss added, "You're a very worthy worker, full of great promise. But the sad truth is that you lack *backbone*."

At that moment, Lee suffered a mental image of that vast aquatic monster deboning one of its fishy victims. He'd once heard it said that sharks tended to avoid eating humans because of the filleting involved; in short, they were unable to remove their skeletons . . . and what part of a person's fundamental framework was more prominent than the *spine*, something Mr Philips, still grinning with obvious relish, had just said Lee lacked?

Now another possibly apocryphal tale occurred to Lee. Somebody had once told him that certain creatures—maybe calves or lambs—were executed after being tenderised by distress, ensuring that their meat was fresher, softer, tastier . . .

And was *this* what the residents of Priory had been doing to him?

He remembered other employees, young men like himself who'd lasted only months in post at the company. Had *they* been invited here, too, before apparently leaving the business with no further word?

"Mrs Links, what *is* this stuff?" asked young Claudia again, but on this occasion, nobody told her what she was eating and Lee didn't give them chance. He stood at once, holding out his almost empty crystal glass for protection. Either its contents had made him paranoid or he was absolutely right to be afraid. Then everyone—all the adults, at least—also climbed to their feet, tongues licking lips after dining on such rare, choice morsels.

"What makes *you* so special?" asked somebody, but Lee, his vision smearing back and forth, was no longer capable of deciding who. Just then, another colossal sound struck up from beneath the building—moist, firm, resonant.

"How dare you question the principles of our *church*?" asked another, and this dramatic switch of focus—from mere community to a hint about organised religion—disturbed Lee. Indeed, he now saw each of the people moving inexorably his way as unquestioning adherents of some dark creed. His eyesight continued swimming in and out of focus. More of those eager, hungry noises from underneath the property—they sounded like growls or maybe the appetite-enlivened belly-protests of an insatiable beast—filled his head with panic. Lee backed away, finally nudging up against an immovable wall. It occurred to him that nobody would know or even care if he went missing; he had no family members he spoke often to, nor close friends or a partner. Perhaps his assailants had factored this into their careful plan. At that moment, Mr Philips, his bullish tone unrelenting, spoke again.

"It's how things are, young man. And alas, you, like so many before you, have fallen short. But that's okay. We like tender. *It* likes tender. And Lord knows that the beast will dine well tonight."

Then—coming rapidly together in Lee's compromised vision, flesh merging with flesh like raindrops rolling down a windscreen—they were all upon him.

THE SUBPRIME

An hour later, deep beneath the same house, eleven guests prepared to observe the community's biannual ritual.

The victim on this occasion hadn't been groomed from the outset. Indeed, Harvey Philips, the homeowner, had held out high hopes for the young man's progress with his finance company. But when the guy's nerve had gone—it was conscience, of course; always their prissy senses of self—he'd unwittingly identified himself as eminently suitable.

The *thing* fed twice a year; Harvey wasn't sure why it needed to eat people in such modest quantities, but that was an issue for greater minds than his own. All he knew was that Charles Erich had put into operation a rota system, with every family living in Priory responsible in turn to find meat.

All the other guests—the Westons, the Simpsons, Mr Johnson and Miss Jeffries—possessed similar opportunities to identify appropriate subjects, making an assessment about the consequences of them vanishing, and then ensuring they arrived on the appointed evening. Nobody had ever failed. It was remarkable just how many dispensable people they were in the world right now.

The room in which the group was now collected was about fifty yards below ground level and accessed by a spiral staircase running from the rear of the house above. It had taken a while to get the victim secured in the metal framework, which would soon be visible behind a large glass window directly up ahead, looking onto a deep, green body of water. This was where *it* resided, the thing that had inspired Erich's great vision, his peerless design for a community so pious it resembled a new religion.

Priory contained images of the beast in many places, but Harvey wasn't sure anybody had ever seen more than fragments of it in the flesh. The distance sketches of the creature certainly offered only a suggestion of its true awesomeness, not unlike an official estimation of the national debt. He and his neighbours had previously observed its great suckered tentacles making short work of sacrificial fodder—just as they would in a moment—but more than this they could only imagine. Perhaps that was for the best.

"Are we all ready?" said Harvey, one hand clutched around a remote-control device, which would set tonight's eagerly awaited event into swift, irreversible action. He'd had a few reserve candidates in line—other men who'd failed to do their worst at the company—but when Lee Mann had recently called to express his doubts, he'd been unable to believe his good fortune. Lee had been good, young, lively and keen. His meat would be fresh, no doubt about that.

"We're ready," came a chorus of salivating responses, the makers sitting one by one on rows of chairs specially installed for this purpose: for the evisceration, the deboning, the extraction of a living man's spine.

Man? Did Harvey really mean *man*? Could a person be described as such without possessing any metaphorical backbone? The concept amused Harvey, adding fun to the task of ensuring survival of his beloved community. He knew Charles Erich would observe the event, having travelled especially from the Ghost House this evening. The man preferred to remain out of sight, at the far back of the room, in a shadowy alcove specifically included for this purpose. He'd always been strong and imperious, but to maintain his formidable reputation, he preferred elusiveness to overly showy demonstrations of power, while engaging with members of Priory only when absolutely necessary. Nevertheless, Harvey knew that the man couldn't remain in charge of the community forever and that a day would come when he'd relinquish his position, handing over the glorious place's reins to a younger, abler person. This might occur many years in the future, but Harvey had always felt that eligibility to succeed Erich needed to be exhibited over time. And surely his performance this evening had done little to damage that developing reputation among his immediate peers.

Harvey pressed the remote control's main button.

Moments later, with silent streams of bubbles and a stirring of green depths, a figure dropped down beyond the thick sheet of glass ahead of the hand-selected crowd. More community residents would have liked to be present, but this group had been chosen on this occasion, mainly because of their professional investments in Priory, in keeping it efficiently operational. Tonight was their treat, a glimpse of their God; indeed, nothing could beat a *live* performance.

The man, strapped rigidly into a rudimentary frame which was suspended from above by a thick chain, had been dressed in a rubber suit, his face covered by a scuba mask. He could breathe via a single oxygen tube strapped to his back, but Harvey doubted the guy saw very much. The liquor distributed before the main course had been harmless except for his employee's glass, to which Harvey had added a drug which induced blurred vision and disorientation. It was likely that its effects remained, perhaps even rendering the man numb as the operation now proceeded without anaesthetic.

The room had grown deathly silent; there was just the figure behind the glass and eleven transfixed onlookers. The man's eyes through the mask blinked sluggishly, as if at some level he knew what fate awaited him. He appeared to look directly at Harvey, but maybe that was just a coincidence.

Then something swooped out from the depths beyond the victim.

It came gracefully, like a delicate leaf unfurling. A paler green than the water, it was clearly a tentacle, but such a strange example of one that it made its audience gasp. A hundred small suckers opened and closed like fish mouths all the way to its tip, from which a number of opaque probes protruded, each long and bonelessly firm. The whole thing—this undoubted limb of some immense entity, almost certainly one of many more— seemed to toy with its offering, circling and sliding around his body, until the blinking eyes beyond that mask snapped urgently shut. Perhaps the toxins in the man's blood were losing hold; maybe terror had triggered a chemical rebalancing, maximising their host's chances of escape.

But that was possible. Indeed, only seconds later, the suckered tentacle with its precision probes skewered its victim directly in the back.

The figure went limp in his metal casement, the chain shaking silently above. The assaulter held him a while, as if continuing to work on his rear side. For a brief period, the man looked like a puppet into which some drunken master had sunk a hand, but that was when the deed was completed. With a single snatching motion, the tentacle snatched out the man's spine, forcing him to crumple immediately, a cloud of redness billowing around him.

The beast had what it wanted: a meal lacking an intrusive spine. Then it tossed away this knuckled vertebrae, making the disconnected strip seesaw downwards. Moments later, it took firm hold of the guy, squeezing with its pale, greenish bulk; those suckered mouths bit at his flesh, as if each was capable of drawing strength from such pink mass. If it hadn't already destroyed his central nervous system, it might have compressed all the air out of him. Indeed, his oxygen tank now exploded with a silent scattering of bubbles.

"Mr Links?" asked the dark-skinned girl near the front of the room, the only child present this evening. Others would attend future events, just as more had directly witnessed similar episodes in the past. It was the community's way of establishing secrets, of ensuring each new generation remained committed to the project; it was an innocence-overruling rite of passage.

"Yes, Claudia?" said Harry, and then Harvey—who, along with his dear wife Barbara, was wilfully childless; offspring was not an expectation of Priory membership—listened keenly to the exchange.

"That stuff we ate earlier, before we all ganged up on that man . . . "

"What about it, young lady?" replied Mrs Links, the finest banker Harvey knew. She'd secured for him a number of major loans during his business's development, turning a blind eye to some of his more immoral ventures.

Then, with the enviable curiosity of everyone lacking responsibilities, the girl asked, "Was it a *man* we ate?"

"Don't be silly, my dear," the woman replied, eagerly watching that tentacle take away its booty, ready to devour. As the limb coiled and lashed a final time, it was possible to see small chunks missing from along its impressive length, as if the slivers of meat its onlookers had enjoyed earlier were mere flesh wounds, like skin scraped from a human finger.

As the invader disappeared, leaving only murky green water, the swiftly extracted spine continued drifting down, down, down.

"But if I were you, Claudia, I wouldn't think too hard about what the dinner plates were made of," Mr Links added in a playful whisper, and his voice had a smirk about it, even though his head was turned away from a now fully satisfied Harvey Philips.

IMPOSSIBLE COLOURS

JAMES EVERINGTON

MICHALA FELT A hand on her shoulder, and as she turned the grey and magnolia corridor seemed to flare in her vision with colours that weren't there.

"Community Officer Bruce," the policeman behind her said, "I'm arresting you for the murder of . . . the murder of . . . "

Michala blinked the colours away; when she opened her eyes Pete was grinning so much he couldn't continue with the joke, whatever it was. He was glancing around the station at the others for approval.

"Pete, get off me," Michala said, swatting his hand away from her uniform. She saw the look in his eyes change and knew the thought behind it: can't take a joke, chip on her shoulder . . . "What are you on about?" she said, not able to help the placatory tone of her voice.

Pete shrugged, looking uncomfortable now his joke had been rebuffed. "That Marty Young. He's dead. And you had motive, right, after that incident up at Priory?

I mean, sorry Michala, it was just a *joke,* I didn't actually think . . . "

"He's dead? Murdered?"

"Nah," Pete said, "racist twat killed himself." He said the r-word uncomfortably—any discussion of race in the Exham police station involving Michala seemed to make the others uncomfortable. Because she was black (or half so; her father was white) and a woman, and just a Community Officer at that. She didn't quite know why, if it was the others who felt uncomfortable, it left *her* feeling the outsider. Not that Pete and the others were racist exactly. Just . . . behind the times, in this backwater. Michala, originally from a large city farther north, made them unsure of themselves and so they made allowances for her she didn't need, and then got defensive when she wasn't grateful.

"He killed himself?"

"Yeah, one of the uniforms was called out because the blood was . . . It came through the ceiling of the tenant below and . . . "

"God. How did he do it?"

"You know I can't tell you that . . . " Pete turned to go and she grabbed his shoulder this time—too short to be real police, too, they sometimes joked, even though that rule hadn't existed for twenty years except in their heads.

"C'mon, Pete, tell me. At least let me know it wasn't quick for the bastard . . . " She didn't really hope that, having found Marty to be pitiful more than anything, but she knew she had to play Pete a bit. Play the race card, despite how she disappointed herself doing so.

"Okay, okay," Pete said, his face colouring. "Just don't tell anyone." He wouldn't meet her gaze as they went to his PC. Maybe the prank arrest had been to hide his real feelings; Michala couldn't help but feel obscurely guilty.

"Fuuuuuuck," she said when she saw the report. "Fuck, he must *really* have wanted to die."

"I know, right?" Pete said. "I pity the poor sods who have to clean up after . . . "

"No note?" Michala said, scanning the screen. "Huh?"

"He didn't leave a note? Someone as keen to share his opinions as that, and he didn't leave a note?"

"Oh don't get all conspiracy theory on me," Pete said. "It's open and shut. Look—no other DNA, no sign of forced entry. Besides, if you were going to fake a suicide, would you really do it like . . . like that?" He nervously closed the report so that she couldn't read it again. "Look, we *know* he was a nutter, why expect it to make sense? *You* know that as well as anyone."

That was true enough, Michala thought, thinking of the odd scene that had taken place outside the gates of Priory with Marty Young and . . . what was his name? Charles Erich.

Priory was an anomaly—technically part of Exham's patch, but they never patrolled there, no officers ventured behind its high white walls. Michala had asked why, of course, but only been given evasive answers (not *real* police . . . the voices in her head had insisted). And she had to admit the religious gated community seemed innocent enough, boring even. No crime was ever reported from it and so the police ignored it. Apart from that day she'd met Marty, and technically that had been outside Priory, anyway.

Michala had walked up the cobbled road leading to Priory's only gates; it had been a few weeks after the clocks had changed, and the evening's light was still a surprise. Priory's walls seemed to glint with minute colours in the fading sun. Despite this she'd been brooding about her place in Exham, in the force overall—her future seemed a series of partial choices all leading nowhere she wanted to be.

She saw a man kneeling at the steel gates of Priory; she'd not realised until now that the gates weren't completely solid, but had a small gap filled with bars which the kneeling man was gripping with both hands as if imprisoned. He had his back to her, so she could see the curve of his spine under his ill-fitting suit, and bubble-gum on the sole of one shoe. His head was bowed.

"Sir?" she said approaching. The man didn't react, not even when she leant in to see his face. It was hard to be sure in the bright golden light but Michala thought his eyes were open but unfocused. "Sir, are you all right?" she said, to no response. She looked at the way the man's hands gripped the bars of the gate so tightly they were white with blood loss; the bars were adorned with strange metal carvings of what Michala took to be octopuses although she wasn't sure.

The man stood, making her step back in surprise. He took a few steps to the side and half-turned to her; when she tried to look at him now it was directly into the low light of the sun and she had to blink the sudden reds and oranges from her sight. The man's eyes were open, she saw, and completely vacant. Or . . . not vacant exactly, but like he was seeing something else. He lifted his right arm, the movement jerky as if a string had just been pulled; his fingers splayed and clenched, as if trying to grip or press something that wasn't there. He took a step forward and reached again for something unseen. Poor sod, Michala thought. She had seen enough substance abuse back home.

She reached out and touched him on the shoulder.

The man flinched and Michala jerked back instinctively; the evening light seemed to intensify in her vision at the contact between the two of them, the shadows of the walls and man himself seeming to twist like the movements of the Op-Art posters she'd had on her walls as a student . . . When she refocused her vision, she saw the man looking at her with eyes that seemed total clear. And contemptuous.

"I was *almost . . .*" he said, then stopped himself. He was a man maybe in his late forties, wearing a faded suit that didn't sit well on his slender frame. The knot of his tie looked too tight under his overly prominent Adam's apple. Michala was reminded of a suspect in court, dressed up to impress the judge. But who was this guy trying to impress?

"Might have known it would be one of *you lot* who stopped me," he muttered.

"My lot?" Michala said. She wasn't sure if he meant the police or something worse. Why she'd assumed the countryside would be less prejudiced than the city she had no idea. When he didn't reply she asked him his name.

"Marty Young," he said, attempting to stand taller as he did so. He looked at her defiantly and then away a second later.

"And why," Michala said, "are you up here? Have you been drinking?" She knew he hadn't, but there must be some explanation for the man's bizarre behaviour earlier, despite his apparent normalcy now.

Just then the gates to Priory started to slide open.

The figure who came through looked superficially similar to Marty Young, but moved with more self-assurance.

"Is there a problem, officer?" the man said to Michala.

"No, no problem," Marty said, before she could speak.

"I found this man at the gates to your . . . where you live," she said. "Is he one of yours? I have reason to suspect he might be drunk or have taken-"

"Who called you, officer?"

"What?"

"I assume someone called you here?" There was a new tone to the man's voice that Michala wasn't sure how to decipher. He had the same snide yet innocent voice Pete and the others used when they tried to wind her up.

And just who had called her?

"You *live* in Priory?" Marty cut in before she remembered.

"I'm Charles Erich," the man replied. Michala saw with amusement how surprised Marty looked, panicked even.

"Because you know, I applied to live in Priory, I sent a letter but no one-"

"We tend to find our recruits in a more . . . informal manner than written application," Erich said. "Not just anyone is let in."

"Yes. Of course. Makes sense," Marty said hastily. "Of course, I'm sure you know I'm not drunk or high or anything. I'm not some dirty addict; not an immigrant."

Oh goody, Michala thought, he's one of *those*. She wondered how many immigrants Marty had ever even seen. The only other non-white faces in Exham belonged to Mr Bhatti and his family who ran the local takeaway, and even they had learned to speak in clipped RP to fit in.

"I bet there's none of *them* allowed to live in Priory, is there?" Marty continued. "The immigrants?" He glanced slyly at Michala. "The coloured?"

"Sir . . . !" she started, but Erich was replying, and despite herself she listened, her face flushing as these two white men debated race in front of her.

"We don't think about it in those terms," Erich said. "We think of it more as . . . the pure and impure."

"Pure and impure, oh I like that," Marty said. "That just about sums it up that does."

Michala wasn't sure Marty had understood.

"Indeed," Erich said dismissively. "Well, perhaps you could both be moving on, since neither of you live here. Yet," he added, and now it had darkened Michala had the odd thought that he looked at each of them in turn rather than just Marty. "So if that will be all . . . " He turned away.

Another successful piece of non-police work, Michala thought sourly.

She and Marty watched as Erich entered a combination into the keypad set into the white wall, and the gate slid open, the strange creatures carved into its bars seeming to swim past in her vision, which was still blurred with oddly coloured after-images.

"Pure and impure," Marty said from behind her, temporarily puffed up with confidence after meeting Erich.

Let it go, Michala thought, turn away, you're used to worse than this . . .

"Mongrels," Marty said, high-pitched like a schoolboy saying a bad word.

She turned back to face him.

"Just because he was a racist doesn't mean he wouldn't leave a note," she said to Pete. "C'mon, admit it—it's odd." When Marty had made his complaint about her, Pete and the others had stood up for her and told Marty if he didn't drop it they'd do him for racial abuse. It turned out Marty Young was known locally, an activist in one of those we're-not-racist-but political parties. He was known for attending Parish meetings demanding action on problems that didn't exist, known for handing out poorly spelt and inaccurate anti-immigration leaflets. But despite every one's support at the station Michala had still felt alone, for had any of them been called mongrels in the street? Until then, they'd all treated Marty as a joke, as just another local eccentric.

So she'd not told them about the second time she'd met him.

"It's unusual," Pete said. "But that's all it is. You've seen the report—you shouldn't have, but you have—it must have been suicide."

"But why? Because he didn't get into Priory?"

"He *did* get in," Pete said.

"He did? But his body was found in his flat." Michala said. "Are you going to investigate them, the Priory people? Erich?"

"No," Pete said tightly. "I mean, he gave a statement. It was nothing to do with Priory."

"But then why did he—"

"God, give it a rest, Michala, I don't know do I? There was no note, there was nothing in his diary . . ." Pete clapped his mouth shut.

"His diary? Pete you never said—"

"Oh fuck. Look, it's just . . . It's evidence of an unsound mind, so it supports suicide. *Very* unsound. Rambling about monsters and tunnels and weird colours . . . "

"Weird colours?" Michala said.

She persuaded Pete to sign out the diary from the evidence room—Alison, who was on the desk, stared at them both with, Michala thought, a touch of contempt.

"Oh don't be so paranoid," Pete said when she mentioned it. She bit her lip, knowing she owed Pete for this. She hadn't actually expected him to do it for her. Maybe he thought she felt guilty about Marty's death? Whatever, he gave her the diary and she read it at her desk and no one questioned her. Rules were a bit more lax in a small station like Exham.

She'd expected a real diary, some kind of leather-bound book with a clasp, but in fact Marty had written in a spiral-bound notebook with a scrawl on the front where he had tried to get his pen to work. His handwriting was cramped and hard to read, particularly the final entries. Had he actually written the entries daily, Michala wondered, or were at least some of them a retrospective attempt to make sense of his thoughts and feelings in the hours leading up to his suicide? She shivered, wondering if as he'd written it he'd already decided the grisly manner in which to kill himself . . .

She started reading from the first entry she could find that mentioned the colours.

14th July:

I'm not sure if it's the heat or the crowds, not sure if I've started getting migraines, but I've been seeing these swirling colours. I don't even know what . . . Red? Green? I don't know, they seem to change to black when I look at them straight on, permanently in the corners of my vision as I lay on my bed with the blind drawn. That's what you're supposed to do with a migraine, right? But it didn't feel like a migraine, didn't even feel unpleasant. It was as if the movement of the colours was urging me upwards, out of bed. I felt the pressure build in my head and then *release* itself (that's the only way I can describe it) into these strange colours, and I yielded to them. Similar to an out of body experience, I guess. It wasn't that I wasn't conscious, it was just my actions and thoughts seemed so insignificant compared to the colours and so I let them in.

I saw myself head to the front door, open it, and step out into the night; the stars increased my feeling of unimportance. The chill I should have felt (I was in my night clothes) didn't seem significant, and the stink of the Paki takeaway across the road didn't rile me like normal (like now). I turned and I guess I knew where I was being led, even before I felt the cobbled road beneath my bare feet.

When I returned to myself—when the colours left me, I should say—I was standing with both hands pressed against the white walls of Priory, about twenty meters away from the gate. I don't know how long I'd been there, for time had been another thing seemingly unimportant, like I'd been seeing myself from the perspective of something for whom the years were just seconds. I stepped away from the walls. There was something unsettling in the aftermath, an empty feeling like a hangover which filled me with a revulsion at the way I'd not been myself. But how can something connected with Priory be bad? I looked to the gate, half expecting . . . But it was closed.

I looked at my right hand—the nails were torn, as if I'd been scratching at the wall. Then I turned to look at the flat, two-coloured world the night had made of everything, and began the long trudge home to the stink and people of Exham.

16th July:

I met him today, met Erich!

He didn't disappoint, and I hope I didn't—but that's the kind of phrase *he* would use. That's how much he impressed me!

But before him, there was *her*.

I was outside Priory again and it was as if those odd colours in my sight were swirling through the gate, animating the strange squid like creatures on the bars, and there was a secret there that I *almost* saw . . . And then there was a touch on my shoulder, and the colours shuddered and seemed to swirl both inside and outside of me, forcing me round to face her before they faded. And when I saw her I was reminded, for a moment, of one of those optical illusions where you see a pretty girl looking one way before blinking and then you see a damn gypsy looking the other . . . As if I was seeing one of her and a multitude, all at the same time, standing behind me. And then the colours were gone and it was just her, standing there in her pretend uniform. She wasn't real police—I know the local lads—but one of those Community Officers. As if the likes of her could ever be part of *our* community! She was a half-caste, or whatever you're meant to call them nowadays. Mixed blood.

"Who called *you* here?" I said. I wasn't doing anything illegal. She didn't seem to understand, and just asked me my name. She looked put out by the fact that I wasn't intimidated by her, and accused me of drinking. I didn't know whether to tell her that *that* wasn't illegal, either, or just to leave because I couldn't stand the slow lazy sound of her voice, when suddenly the gate to Priory started to slide open. Maybe I was still seeing the colours for it took me a few seconds to recognise the man who stepped out as Charles Erich. He's not as tall as I thought, but his skin is pale and chalky looking like the walls, and he has that *natural* authority, that way of holding himself that is so rare nowadays. He looked at us both, taking stock of the situation.

"Is there a problem, *officer*?" he said, managing to emphasise that word in a way that showed what he really thought about her uniform.

She started accusing me of being drunk again and Erich listened patiently—too patiently—before interrupting her.

"You *live* in Priory?"—the stupid woman didn't even know who he was.

"I've applied to live there, too," I said, as much for her benefit as his.

"Indeed," Erich said, looking at me. "Well I'm sure ... " He stopped himself. "We have to go through the process obviously. Not just anyone is let in."

"Not the immigrants," I said—more of a statement than a question. I glanced at the gawping Community Officer. "Not the . . . " But there was no need to state what I meant; Erich understood.

"We don't think of it in quite those terms," he said. "We think of it as more the pure and impure."

And isn't *that* just about perfect! The pure and impure!

"Well," Erich said, "perhaps you could both be moving on, since neither of you live here. Yet," he added, and how that gave me hope. "So if that will be all . . . " He turned away, and entered a combination into the keypad set into the white wall, and the gate slid open, and I vaguely wondered what the squid-things were meant to symbolise for the people who lived inside Priory. Similar to the Christian fish?

She just watched him—I thought she'd been dying to say something about his calling her 'impure,' but because of the way he'd only implied it she didn't have a leg to stand on. But her type have to expel their emotions sometimes, it's beyond their control, and she turned to me (I was still watching Erich move away on the other side of the gate) and called me a "racist fucking arsehole."

It was hard for me not to react, of course, and eventually the real police—the white police—were called out. I could see they were sick of this woman, treated her as something of a joke, a burden. We'll do you for racial harassment, they said grinning, practically tapping the side of their noses. I played along and soon they left with me still at large, much to the half-caste's frustration no doubt . . .

Strange, though, what I felt when she touched me. As if some of those weird, squirming colours had *moved* from me to her . . . ***Michala wasn't sure what to make of what she'd just read. Even on the page his distaste for her made her feel sick, as did his suggestion that Pete and the rest were more tolerant of his views than they let on. Brief tears in her eyes made the yellows of the overheard lights swirl, and she saw Alison staring at her from across the room. She gave a tentative smile but the woman just kept staring. Bitch, Michala thought, looking away first.

She supposed she should be glad her confrontation with Marty didn't seem to have been the trigger for any feelings of depression that might have led to his suicide (if it had been suicide—Michala was still keeping an open mind). But then, if Marty wasn't being honest, even to himself, how would she know?

She flipped forward.

$$*$$

21st July:

I saw her again in the street today. I mean obviously she stands out and I almost crossed the road to avoid her, but something stopped me. There's something about those colours, something about the way they move and leave me feeling so trivial . . . It's unnerving. I have doubts I suppose. And this morning I was feeling hemmed in and frustrated by all the people who'd come to Exham for the market. I hate the way there's occasionally a random surge in the crowd and you're forced in a direction you don't want to go, like being forced down a tunnel.

And I remembered the odd feeling of connection when she'd brought me back to myself, and wondered if she'd seen the colours, too.

I stopped her in the street; it was in public and she was in her uniform so how could she refuse? She looked more surprised than angry, there was no visible sign of her controlling her emotions; she *is* half-white I suppose.

"Officer," I said, to show I wasn't going to make a scene. "Could I talk to you about something? About Priory?" I hadn't meant to express it in those terms, but that's how it came out.

"Of course, sir," she said—like we were both playing a role for the benefit of those walking past, and again despite myself I felt some connection because weren't we both in on the same joke? But then a figure stumbled against me in the crowd and I staggered; I had the horrible feeling I was about to be swept away by them all before I steadied myself.

"Sir?" she said, concerned.

"I'm all right"—I flinched away from her, not wanting her to touch me. Her eyes hardened. I wasn't sure how to proceed, wasn't sure how to phrase it so I just blurted it out. Straight up asked her if she'd been seeing strange colours since she'd touched me near Priory.

She looked surprised again and for a second . . . But no, she said no. Looked at me like I was some drunken lunatic (I had had a whisky at lunch). I felt annoyed with myself; why had I expected the likes of her to be able to see what I see?

Except I can, Michala thought. She didn't know why she hadn't admitted it at the time, but the sight of Marty lurching out of the crowd at her had made her defensive, and the way he'd looked, the way he'd spoken—she hadn't assumed him drunk as much as *ill*. She had just hoped he wouldn't touch her.

But she did see the colours, although maybe not as strongly as Marty. No trances, but there was a faint tug when she saw them, a pull of her thoughts towards Priory.

IMPOSSIBLE COLOURS

29th July:

Of course, the colours are impossible to recall when you're not seeing them, impossible to believe anything could be real other than the brown of the terraced houses and the grey of Exham's roads. The pale faces of the crowd; and not always so pale it seems nowadays. Even here there's no escape. I must get away; I must get into Priory.

I haven't been to sign on for weeks, for I get so little sleep at night and the night walks leave me susceptible to illness. They will stop my benefits soon but it is hard to care. I have heard some people gain admittance to Priory merely by the size of their financial contribution, but that way is not open to me. I will have to gain entry another way, by proving my faith and trust in Priory.

Faith, yes that's the word.

How can I prove my faith?

1st August:

Paki bastard had it coming to him.

I've seen him leave that takeaway across the street, taking deliveries on that Moped of his. Why anyone wants to eat their muck is beyond me. And what his parents don't know is sometimes he's a little slower getting back, because he and his girlfriend—his *white* girlfriend—sneak down the alley besides the takeaway, which is always deserted.

I followed them tonight. That traitorous little slut of a girlfriend screamed and called the police before I could do too much damage but . . . Paki bastard had it coming to him.***God, Michala thought, that had been *Marty?* Exham was such a small station everyone knew when a serious crime had been reported, even her, and so she knew enough details to call up the report.

Vikam Bhatti and his finance Sophie Dee had indeed been accosted on the streets round the back of the Viceroy takeaway—as Bhatti told it, a figure they'd first taken to be a beggar had been following them, mumbling something. They'd assumed he wanted money and stopped to give him some change, when he'd flung himself at Bhatti. "It was just embarrassing," Bhatti said in the report. "He slapped at me and the first time I was too surprised to stop him, it was like being slapped by a child—he was that weak, you know? And he stank. He had on a shirt and tie, like those old guys, you know, but it was grubby. I grabbed his wrists to stop him and I could hold them together in one hand. I think he was a sick man, a very sick man. Do you think I need shots?"

Bhatti hadn't wanted the hassle of pressing charges; the matter had only come to the police's attention because Sophie Dee had called for an ambulance because she was so concerned for the man, but he'd fled before it came. No one had really bothered following the incident up, it had been assumed the assailant was an outsider, an itinerant, because the description matched no one they knew in Exham. Typical small station mentality, Michala thought, but she could understand why no one had associated the description with Marty. He'd been skinny when she'd met him, and his suit had seen better days, but she'd assumed him the type who'd be ashamed to let himself go. But obviously something had changed.

And if Pete was right, he made it into Priory, she thought. In *that* state?

5th August:

I knew all I needed was to show my faith.

The colours have grown stronger, more vibrant ever since I showed that Paki lad who was boss. Or rather, the rest of life's colours seem drabber and static. The impossible colours *move* and I see shapes in them, just like you do in clouds. Strange animals, weird fishes.

Last night, when the colours faded, one of those shapes remained, dull and grey and tiny but *there.* One of the squid things in the bars of the gates of Priory; I was on my knees with my face practically pressed up to the wrought-iron.

My eyes adjusted and I realised what I could see beyond the bars—the cobbled road that led down into Exham. I was inside looking out. It took me a few seconds to understand; I'd assumed I'd been gripping the bars in frustration at being denied entry, not . . . I spun around. Two men stood behind me in the gloom. I recognised one of them.

"Hello again," said Charles Erich.

"I'm . . . You let me in?" I said. I was aware I wasn't exactly dressed for the occasion; I'd taken to sleeping in my clothes because of the night journeys the colours led me on, and they were crumpled and shapeless. I couldn't remember when I'd last changed them or showered.

"You were let in," Erich said. "These things are not always decided by us, and as Mr Philips here has reminded me the reasons are not always clear." The other man just grunted.

"I haven't . . . I haven't much in the way of a donation," I said, but Erich waved me silent.

"Not all who come here are chosen because of wealth," he said, "but . . . "

"But because they're *pure*?" I said, remembering his word that day. Erich stared at me; Mr Philips laughed and wrinkled his nose.

"Maybe you were right, Mr Philips," Erich said, then more loudly, "This is Mr Philips, he often works late so I knew he'd be awake when I became aware you'd be . . . admitted. Mr Philips will show you to one of our empty dwellings. We will decide what's best in the morning."

Before I could reply Erich left the courtyard, his dark clothes making him vanish as soon as he turned. The man called Mr Philips gestured me to follow him; his manner was polite but reserved, as if I were someone he'd know only fleetingly rather than someone he'd now see every day. Maybe he was just annoyed that his work had been interrupted.

IMPOSSIBLE COLOURS

He led me away from the courtyard and the white outer walls, up the main street of Priory—the streets are laid out in symmetrical patterns it seems, identical Y-shaped junctions at regular intervals. Each street is lined with identical looking bungalows with low white picket fences. It all looked so strange and peaceful in the moonlight; there were no lights on in the bungalows and everything was silver-edged. There were no numbers or street names, and the house Mr Philips led me to had nothing to distinguish it from all the rest.

He opened the front door without unlocking it—of course they have no need to protect themselves from criminals and immigrants here. Inside it was more spacious than I'd imagined, or just more empty maybe, with white walls and minimalist store bought furniture.

Mr Philips, not looking at me, said they'd arrange for any clothing and sundries I wanted from my flat to be brought here. I could tell he was itching to go, but before he did I pointed out of one window:

"What's that?" I said, for the building I could see, which I guessed must be at the centre of Priory, was taller than all the others. It was white stone with a roof of sloped black slate; it looked old, as if it had always been there, and the bungalow I was stood in seemed a flimsy and transient thing in comparison.

Mr Philips shrugged. "That's Erich's house," he said. I didn't even turn around as he left. Erich's house! I feel privileged; only a few of the bungalows would be close enough to have an unobstructed view of Erich's home; there *is* something to distinguish mine after all.

6th August:

I slept through most of the day, until I was woken up by Mr Philips, who told me he was to take me to Erich's house. The clothes and other items from my flat had already arrived and so I hurriedly dressed and followed him. All the streets of Priory converge and lead towards Erich's house; a few of my fellow residents glanced at me as we passed but none made eye contact. I suppose, to them, I have yet to prove my place here, but there was nothing appraising in their looks, just a . . . blankness, I suppose. Or is it just a lack of tension? For *I* still feel tense, I can't help it, still feel I am in danger of being overrun.

Erich was waiting for us on the doorstep; we didn't go inside. *His* look was appraising alright. He looked at me without speaking for what seemed a long time.

"I'm still of the same opinion, Mr Philips," he said eventually.

"Why rush judgement?" Mr Philips said. Erich turned to me.

"Are you a religious man?" he said.

"No, I . . . I mean I know you are here and I want to learn, but . . . "

"You'll see our church, soon enough," Erich said. "Myself and Mr Philips just disagree about in what . . . capacity."

"Where *is* the church? I've not seen a spire or . . . "

"Our temple is underground," Erich said.

"Underground?"

"Yes, safe from prying eyes above." I knew *exactly* who he meant. "There's tunnels," Erich continued, "which run from every home in Priory to the temple. At Mr Philips's insistence, access to the one under your house has been locked until we decide what's best. It's not every day we get someone who arrives in the manner you did."

I tried to ignore what he said about Mr Philips; the man really doesn't like me for some reason. "The colours led me," I said.

"People are led here for . . . various reasons," Erich said.

"What *are* they?" I said. "The colours?" I didn't quite know how to express what I meant.

"Impossible colours," Erich said, "that's what the scientists call them. Have you ever looked at an optical illusion, or at the sky for too long, and seen colours behind your eyes afterwards? They're created in our minds, and our minds sometimes create colours that can't exist, according to scientists, that couldn't exist on any physical spectrum of light." He made a scoffing noise. "But what do scientists know, eh Mr Philips?"

"I'm not a physicist," Mr Philips said gruffly.

"But I don't just see them when my eyes are closed," I said. "And now I am *here* so why can I still see . . . "

"That," Erich said, "is what we all want to know."

7th August:

This morning I found someone had been into my house while I slept and left food and other essentials in the cupboards. Is it wrong to feel slightly uneasy that they came inside without me realising? A hangover from my old life, no doubt.

I wondered if I would get to see the church today. I don't actually know much about their religion here—some offshoot of Christianity, I suppose, that they've had to adopt because the CoE and Catholics are so infiltrated by the lesser races, singing and clapping . . . But I have no need to think such things anymore, no need to let it get to me. I can shed the bile and helpless nausea; I am safe.

This morning I felt at a loss what to do. Instinct—my instinct, not that of the colours—urged me towards Erich's house, but I worried about pestering him and so I headed in the opposite direction towards the gate. Some of the other residents came and went as I watched—there was some kind of code they entered to open the gate. How did I get through that night? I had been so caught up in the excitement of being inside Priory that I hadn't considered the *how*. How had I known the code? I tried to recapture the feeling of seeing the colours and wondered if then I *had* known it, or if whatever I felt a small part of had known . . .

I certainly don't know it now; I will have to ask Erich when I see him. It is obviously unintentional, but I am a virtual prisoner without it. I suppose I could have asked one of the people this morning, but something about the vacant looks they wore made me disinclined to speak to them. I mean, I know if was just an early morning routine for them, but still . . . Something about the blank-eyed way they entered the combination made me reluctant.

Eventually I went back to the house and lay on the sofa just dozing. The colours came as my eyes closed; it was as if they were just waiting for me to relax to begin sliding over me, pulling at me, urging me to go where they led . . .

I came to and for a second the thoughts that remained in my head were alien and incomprehensible, one voice and many somehow simultaneously. I found myself on my knees and from the stiffness in my joints I must have been so for some time. I was in the small study at the back of the house, a room I'd not really paid much attention to, for there was little there save an empty bookshelf, a desk, and the frayed rug I was kneeling on. Its faded swirling patterns were like an after-image of the colours, and that realisation seemed to trigger them to swirl up around me again. Erich is right, these impossible colours cannot just be products of the mind, for how could the mind create something new?

Observing from without, I saw myself stand and pull up the rug, revealing a trapdoor beneath.

The entrance to the tunnels, I thought—or rather, heard someone think. I knelt down again and saw that the padlock attached to the trapdoor bolt was one that required a combination of numbers to open. My hands seemed distant, detached things in the improbable hues, and when they turned the first cylinder to 9 I didn't know who it was who knew that number. Nor when they turned the second to 4 and the third to 4 and . . .

And then the colours fled, and reality reasserted itself and my own thoughts seemed slow and one-dimensional. 944 . . . something. There were only ten possible combinations it could be; it would take less than a minute to try them all. I thought about the church that was underground, how magnificent it must be; I pictured it carved into white stone.

I was about to try the first combination when I heard sounds from beneath the trapdoor. Footsteps, lots of them, in time. Everyone else going to worship at the underground church, I thought. Hadn't Erich said the tunnels ran from every house? I thought about opening the trapdoor and joining them, but the thought of sneaking around like I didn't belong annoyed me. Besides, there was something disturbing about the sound. Maybe it was the lack of voices from below, the lack of any variation in their synchronised footfalls. I imagined they looked as vacant as the people I had watched at the gate earlier . . . and as vacant as I, no doubt, had looked when the colours had led me to this room.

I let the padlock fall and turned away; I tried to busy myself with other things as the sound of footsteps faded . . .

Two hours later, I heard them all return in unison, too.

8th August: [They found his body the next day, Michala thought. This was Marty Young's last day alive.]

Sod that smug Mr Philips. Sod him and the way he looks at me, the way his nose automatically wrinkles like I'm still wearing the same clothes! They called me to see them again, outside Erich's house; as I neared Erich was saying something about "sacrifice" and Mr Philips was shaking his head. As if doubting my commitment to Priory and what I'd give up for it.

They asked me about the colours again and for some reason I didn't want to tell them they'd led me towards the trapdoor and almost showed me the combination. So instead I told them about why I had wanted to come into Priory, of the feeling that my world is being overrun with those I despise . . .

The way he *laughed*. The way Mr Philips laughed at me; I thought it would be different in here! I've met his type before when handing out leaflets or in Parish meetings, 'liberals' who use the charge of racism as just another way to look down at people like me.

And Erich didn't even chastise him.

So sod him—I don't know how he's got influence over Erich and the whole thing might be a test, anyway. Sod them.

After I've heard the footsteps return and I know the tunnels are empty, I'm opening the trapdoor tonight.

Later:

I have to get out of Priory, I have to get out.

I've dragged the desk and bookshelf over the trapdoor and I've locked it. It's madness, obviously, to stay here for thirty minutes writing this, but there has to be some record. Thank goodness my notebook was one of the things they brought from my flat. Not that I know who will ever read this; the only one I can think of is *her*. A strange thought: that half-caste might be the only person I can trust.

Maybe, if I can get out, the colours will stop? A big 'if'—my only hope is that the combination for the main gate is the same they used for the trapdoor. But given what I've seen tonight that's not as unlikely as it sounds, even if the combination was set by another person. The colours will be of no help getting out for they are insistent in pulling me the other way, towards the trapdoor … The way they move! I have been using words such as 'swirling', but really, the colours move in my eyes like tentacles, sliding over each other.

So I must write down what happened whilst I have the willpower. If I don't escape there's at least a chance she will see this, for if I *can't* get out I'd rather kill myself than … And that surely will bring the police into Priory?

Oh god.

I must hope to escape but write this in the expectation that I will fail:

I raised the trapdoor—the combination was 9441, the first I tried—and I saw steps down into a passageway. I cautiously descended, making sure the trapdoor couldn't swing shut behind and trap me—and thank god I did. The tunnel was obviously old, the stone below my feet worn so smooth it was almost slippery. I wondered how many feet had worn it so, over the years. The walls and ceiling were rougher, carved from what stone I didn't know, but it was something that reflected tiny glints of light—I didn't need Erich to tell me the light was of a colour no scientist would say possible. The tunnel was also lit by infrequent dusty, low-watt lights attached to the sides of the walls.

There was a slight incline so I walked downwards. The tunnel joined others but they were all converging rather than separating so I was never unsure which direction to go in. I stopped every few seconds to listen, telling myself I was being paranoid. I told myself this so repeatedly that it took me a while to realise that I could hear something behind me, after all.

I was at a Y-shaped junction with another tunnel when I realised what I could hear were footsteps, coming from the passage I had just come down. I wondered if I could get back to the trapdoor to my house (I still thought of it as mine, then) by going up the other tunnel behind me. In deliberating, I realised footsteps could be heard from that tunnel, too.

I moved quickly then, running downwards. At the next point where two tunnels converged I turned to the other but heard more footsteps; at each potential point of turning back it was the same. The footsteps were slow, not running but walking as if in sync, even from different tunnels. Like I was being herded towards the underground church. Why had they kept me from it, if now they were trying to force me towards it?

I stopped, thinking I was letting my old modes of thought affect me. These weren't immigrants or thieves to be frightened of, these were the people of Priory. Why was I assuming they were a threat? Maybe I'd passed some kind of test by coming down here and everyone was to join me and Erich for some kind of initiation. That would show Mr Philips! I almost laughed out loud at my stupidity—as if the nightly sounds of footsteps in the tunnels hadn't been clue enough!

I continued walking forwards and downwards, still hearing the slow tread of footsteps at every turn behind me, getting louder as more and more people converged in the same passageways. I couldn't hear any talking or laughter, just their footsteps all in time.

I turned a corner and found myself in a semi-circular space about twenty metres wide; there was one of the electric lights attached to one wall and at the far end a carved archway. Cautiously, I walked through the arch. The chamber on the other side was poorly lit, the colours having deserted me. I could feel damp in the air and hear the dripping of water; something about the way the sound echoed convinced me I was in a large space. As my eyes adjusted to the gloom I thought I saw movement; I heard soft wet sounds which the echoes made seem were everywhere in front of me.

I called out Erich's name.

Something came towards me and I shrieked—a pallid, eyeless thing with a spread of tentacles around a wet O of a mouth; its body in the gloom behind it seemed limbless, like just a bigger tentacle itself. Despite its open mouth it was silent apart from the wet sounds of its movement. It jerked oddly as another one of the things emerged beside it, and another to the other side as if trying to encircle me.

The way they moved was like they were one thing not many, as if what I took to be their white, colourless bodies were merely larger tentacles converging in the same way as the tunnels I had come down, leading back to even thicker tentacles leading back to . . .

I flung myself back through the archway—the things moved towards me but then stopped and fell back, exactly like a giant hand that couldn't reach far enough.

Back out I turned to run but then stopped, appalled—the footsteps were very loud now, marching down the single tunnel that led to this antechamber; everything converged here. There was no other way out. The residents of Priory came into the antechamber, all of them blank-eyed and silent, and I thought at first they meant by sheer weight of numbers to force me backwards into the large space where the wet, pallid things (thing?) waited to enfold me. But they merely spread out and stood looking at me. They weren't expressionless, but all wore the same expression, like they were all thinking the same thing at the same moment. Or one thing was thinking the same thing inside each of them.

Charles Erich stepped from the crowd.

"So you've seen our church?" he said, gesturing to the arch behind me. That place with that horror inside is your *church?* I thought. "Unorthodox," Erich continued, "but then everything about your arrival has been unorthodox. But you have *seen.*" His face was rapturous.

I wondered, if the colours had been with me when I had seen it, whether my face would have been rapturous, too?

"The colours led you here," Erich said. "I must admit I was wrong, I thought your arrival merely foreshadowed another. But you must give yourself up to His touch. We will go back in and complete your purification." He straightened up as if getting ready, and everyone else in the room except me did so, as well. Then they all took a step forward simultaneously and I thought that here, now, they were all as much one being as those pale and monstrous tentacles at my back. And if they forced me back inside and I felt its embrace then I would be part of it, too. I would have joined Priory.

They took another step, then another, slowly moving forward and leaving me with less and less space as I was forced backwards toward the archway . . .

And I realised part of me, the part that had seen the colours, wanted this, wanted to be lost in something bigger and purer than myself.

With what felt like the last of my willpower, I darted to the side and pulled the electric light from the wall, then smashed it to the ground. Erich cried out in anger. In the sudden darkness I heard the scrambling of the tentacles in the church behind me grow more frantic, not wanting to be denied.

Immediately the mob of bodies pushed forwards; I felt them brush either side of me, felt hands reach out blindly for me, grabbing for my clothes, my hair. I tried to push through them in the commotion but realised it was hopeless, there were so many of them and I was disorientated. I felt the deep horror of being subsumed in the crowd well up in me . . .

Hands found me, but they pulled not pushed me, slammed me against the opposite wall. One of my hands hit bare rock but one reached out and found I was at the entrance to the tunnel I had come down . . .

IMPOSSIBLE COLOURS

"Go that way," Mr Philips whispered in my ear.

Quickly, too scared to wonder if I was making a noise, I fled up the tunnel. The sporadic lighting barely illuminated it and I realised how much I'd been relying on the impossible colours for light as I'd come the opposite way. And of course the tunnels were splitting now not converging, and I had to choose which to run up, relying on instinct. How likely was it I would make the right decision at every fork? I was close to despair again, for when the mob realised I'd escaped and came back up the tunnels hunting me, I'd have no chance. Mr Philips would not help me if it meant revealing his treachery to others. But then I saw a soft, yellow light ahead of me—the trapdoor to my house, which I'd left open.

Whimpering with relief I scrambled back up the steps, slammed the lid down, and reattached the padlock with trembling hands.

But I have wasted too much time writing this. If anything happens to me, I can only hope she finds this record—I don't even recall her name. *But she didn't see the colours.* She told me so. Maybe only we whites are debased enough to see them.

And now I can only hope that the people of Priory think so much alike that they have used the same combination on all of their locks, including the gate.

That was the last entry, although Michala saw that the next two pages of the spiral bound notebook had been torn out. God, she thought, Pete was right, Young really had been insane. It was like all his hatred at the outside world had suddenly snapped back on himself. And how had he come to be so fixated on *her*?

His body had been found at his flat, Michala thought, so he did make it out of Priory. Assuming the whole thing wasn't delusion. His description of his encounters with Vikam Bhatti and Michala herself had certainly been inaccurate, so how could she trust any of it? Never mind the bits about the tentacled monsters. Monster. Michala had her doubts that a community like Priory would ever have admitted someone like Marty, the state he'd been in. Still, she supposed Marty had one advantage over her; she had no doubt one thing from his diary was accurate—that everyone who got into Priory was white.

Obsessed, you're obsessed, she thought. She closed her eyes wearily but the colours that swirled behind her lids were no relief.

Marty was right, she thought, they do move like tentacles.

She shook her head as if to throw such thoughts from her, and headed towards the evidence room. "I'm returning it for Pete," she said to Alison, who stared at her.

"I won't say anything," Alision said.

"What?"

"I won't say anything. I don't want to get him into trouble."

"Okay," Michala said tiredly, turning to go. She knew Alison had never liked her.

"He used to see a girl from round here you know," Alison said suddenly. "Local girl. Very pretty. Good family. He took it hard when they split up."

"What? Why are you telling me this?"

"Just saying, a local girl's good enough for some is all."

"You're warning me off? But Pete doesn't . . . " Michala didn't finish.

"That Marty Young maybe wasn't wrong about *everything*," Alison said levelly.

Don't say anything, don't say anything—Michala turned away. She knew Pete had signed the diary out for her, she owed it to him not to react. Never mind her own career. For what that was worth; she again thought of every decision she made leading to the same dead end.

You will never be allowed to fit in here, she thought.

Pete? she thought.

But she'd stayed so long reading the diary that the jacket was already gone from the back of his chair.

On the drive home she passed Priory, a white shape against the sunset in the distance. 9441, she thought, if Marty got out then that's what the combination must be. If I went up there and tried it and the gate didn't open then obviously the whole thing's bollocks and there's no need for further investigation into Priory's role in his death. But if she tried it and the gate opened . . . Then, well, it's probably *still* bollocks, she told herself.

9441—the first step towards doing something was visualising it, she knew, and she felt herself so encircled by the strange, nameless colours in her vision she could almost see her hand rising to enter the numbers. But she was stronger than Marty, she wouldn't give in to the faint but insistent urge towards Priory in her thoughts.

At least wait until morning she told herself.***Who called you here? Michala thought as she stared at the keypad next to the gate to Priory. She had never answered. She had never known, that day when she met Marty.

She'd not been to the station first, wasn't even in her uniform, and her early morning decision to come here seemed a hazy and dream-like thing. The colours moved in her vision, bursting forth like from an underground tunnel before pulling back. But had the colours really led her here, or was that just part of Marty's bullshit, and had she really come because she thought his death suspicious and wanted to impress the others? How could a colour be 'impossible' when she could see it, and it was just an after-image from the early morning sun, anyway?

"Sod it," she said aloud, and pressed 9441 on the keypad. Of course it won't work, he was *crazy*, she thought.

There was a pause, and then slowly the gate to Priory slid open.

Unclear if it was what she herself wanted to do, she walked inside.

There was a central courtyard with straight streets leading away from it; she didn't know which would lead to Erich's house so she just picked one at random. The one which was the brightest lit in her vision. It was lined with identical looking bungalows. So he must have been inside, she thought, that at least seems true. There was no one around and the place was eerily quiet other than her footfalls. She reached a Y-shaped junction and didn't know which way to proceed—the streets looked identical. So she picked one at random, and did the same at the next junction, and the next. The still rising sun flared in her vision.

When she stopped at the next junction she became aware of the sound of footsteps behind her.

She looked behind her and saw a crowd of at least twenty people on the path behind her, having merged from the various forks in the road. None of them were speaking and there was a synchronicity to their movements. And a calmness, Michala thought, a warmth in the soft golden light. And if their faces all seemed the same then maybe it was just that old joke—don't all white people look the same to you? But her heart wasn't in it, and wasn't she half-white herself? Although she didn't like to admit it she felt as out of place and unsure of herself with everyone, no matter their race.

"Officer," a familiar voice said; Charles Erich stepped forward. "Who has called you here this time?"

"I'm here about Marty Young," she said, in lieu of anything else.

"Him? Such a shame. But he chose to be an outsider."

Michala snorted. "In my experience, that's not how things work. You don't *choose* to be an outsider, people cast you in that role. Cast you out."

"Not at Priory," Erich said.

"Not at . . . ? It's a *gated community*."

"We have . . . selection criteria," Erich said, "But once you're one of us, you never have to feel an outsider again."

"And what are those 'selection criteria?'" Michala said loudly. "I know, the 'pure and impure,' right? Well excuse me if I've heard that kind of language before. *A lot.*" She took a deep breath, blinked rapidly like she couldn't see properly. She was self-consciously aware of all the people watching her, not saying anything, having all come out of their houses as if hearing the same call . . . And when she looked at the swelling crowd she saw there *were* some black faces, after all. How had she not seen them? How had *Young* not seen them? Yet more proof that he probably hadn't even been inside Priory, she thought, as she glanced at the two faces and away again. She told herself that just because they didn't look threatening didn't mean they weren't; that the welcome on their faces might be false.

"But I haven't come here to debate," she said angrily. "I need to see the house Marty stayed in."

"You found it," Erich said, gesturing to the nearest bungalow.

"Are there . . . Inside, are there any tunnels?" she said, and felt stupid. She was meant to be doing some actual real police work and here she was babbling about tunnels! Of course there weren't tunnels, or underground churches, or a monster.

"Tunnels?" Erich said blandly.

"It's a simple question so . . . "

"It could be yours," Erich said.

"What?"

"It could be yours. You could join us. Isn't that why you're really here?"

"I'm investigating Marty's death," Michala said, too loudly. "And besides, I'm hardly your sort, am I?" But it rang false in her head, knowing the two black faces were behind her.

"We're really not like that," Erich said. "Not like Marty. We know what he didn't. Have you thought that perhaps the only reason he was led here was to pave the way for you?" Erich moved up the path to the bungalow and opened the front door, which was unlocked.

You should leave here now, Michala thought, you're stupid even to consider it. Join some cult? But then, she had to go inside the house, anyway, to investigate—investigate some poor sod's death at his own clumsy hand. She looked at the people behind her, all smiles—there could be no chance these people were involved in Marty's death. They all look the same because they're all *happy*, she thought. She turned and looked through the door Erich was holding open—she could see the inside of the bungalow and its colours clearly, when surely it should be dark from the closed curtains?

Remember Marty thought he was getting what he wanted here, too, a fading part of her brain struggled to say, and she shuddered momentarily despite the heat; a shudder that shook her whole body as if something underground were shuddering below her.

Pete? she thought.

Erich was still holding the door open. "Shall we?" he said.

"I expect *you* know where she is?" Alison said to Pete. "Community Officer Bruce?"

"Michala?" Pete said. "No, I've been looking for her all—"

"This came for her." Alison handed him a slim brown envelope. "But I suppose it should go to a proper officer first, anyway." She sniffed and looked disapproving.

"What is it?" Pete said, opening the envelope. Inside were three sheets of paper torn from a spiral-bound notebook.

"His suicide note," Alison said. "Marty. He sent it directly to *her*. Second class," she added. "Did *he* have a thing for her, as well?"

"Huh?" said Pete, but he was already opening the pages flat so he could read them.

I'm seeing the colours again the first line said, *and now I know where they want to lead me.* As he tried to read further, the writing became less and less legible, and he was aware of Alison standing watching him, waiting to take it back to the evidence room. After all, it was a closed case.

Occasional phrases were legible:

. . . thinking its thoughts; that's what he meant by pure . . .

No wonder the other races hate us; we are different, we are empty vessels . . .

Burn it, burn it to the ground.

"God, he really was mental," Pete said to Alison and saw her frown; he knew she had frequented some of the same meetings Marty had.

The last paragraph of Marty Young's note was slightly clearer, perhaps in recognition that he was near the end:

I had hoped to flee somewhere where I wouldn't see them, but the colours are stronger than ever and I know I will succumb eventually if I live. And I know now what they will lead me to; I know now what belonging at Priory means.

So enough. I must make an end of myself before I weaken. The world will not miss one more white man.

He killed himself because he was white? Pete thought. But the whole note was as crazy as the rest of his diary, and didn't alter the case; he had been delusional and killed himself.

"So where is she?" Alison said, taking the note back off him. "Should I show it to her?"

"I don't know," Pete said, the first beginnings of worry in his voice.

"I'm not sure how long she'll last here," Alison said.

Pete almost argued, but the colours of his coming headache were bright and flared in his vision. He hated to admit it, but she'd barely even acknowledged him so why should he care?

"You're right," he said. "She's never really fitted in has she? Hard to imagine a place where she would."

STOLEN FROM THE SEA

STEPHEN BACON

RYAN MET NATALIE the year before his son's death. It was late one Friday afternoon. He was making his way through the hills that surrounded Exham, heading back into town after a week on the road. He spotted her walking along the roadside, pushing a mud-spattered bicycle with some difficulty. Its two flat tyres were causing the wheels to judder against the sandy ground. Since they'd built the bypass the roads threading through the hills had become deserted; seeing a woman out here alone was somewhat disconcerting. He pulled over and wound down his window.

"Heading into town?" He saw the sweat glistening on her brow, the redness of her cheeks. She was breathing heavily.

"Yeah."

"Want a lift? I'm going that way."

He could see the relief in her face. He hopped out of the car and helped her stow her bike in the back. "I must've run over some glass up on that trail back there," she said apologetically. "Talk about rotten luck! At least it's downhill back into town."

They both climbed into the car. "Still a good few miles though," he said. "Quite a walk."

He noticed her throw a sidelong glance at the wedding ring on his left hand. Its presence seemed to reassure her. She blew out her cheeks. "Yeah, I suppose it'll be getting dark soon. Good job you came past really."

"I prefer to cut through the hills. The bypass is a quick road but it's always busy with traffic." He started the ignition and they set off again. The scrub brush and forlorn-looking trees seemed to watch them from the swiftly-gathering shadows.

She glanced at the pamphlets and boxes of stationary on his back seat. "You a salesman then?"

"Kind of." He studied her surreptitiously through the wing mirror. She had an elfin nose, nice cheekbones, a pair of rosy cheeks that accentuated her freckles. Her dark hair was gathered together in a loose ponytail. He could smell the coconut aroma of her shampoo.

"You live in Exham then?"

"Yes," he said. "You?"

"Hmmm, for now at least. I'm looking for a place of my own. Just renting at the minute." She wrinkled her nose to illustrate her distaste.

His mobile phone beeped, its chime announcing the receipt of a new text message. "Just be my wife," he said. "Wondering where I am."

"Sorry if I've made you late."

"Oh no, don't worry." He smiled at her. "It'll be our son, Ben, wanting to know what time I'll be back. There's a Lego set half-finished."

"How old is your boy?"

"Six."

"Ah, lovely." He could feel the weight of her glance. "I'm Natalie, by the way."

He shook her hand firmly. "Nice to meet you, Natalie. I'm Ryan."

The next year passed in a whirl.

The old man was fidgeting like a child. Ryan stared ahead through the windscreen, but caught occasional glimpses of the man tugging at the collar of his shirt. His chest was rising and falling with some effort.

The car negotiated the busy streets, drawing closer to their destination. The distinct chimneys of Priory rose above the surrounding buildings like a beacon. He turned onto the cobbled street that led up to a rather grand wrought-iron gate. The old man peered out of the side window, gaping in awe at the high perimeter wall and the intricately patterned fence.

"So as you can see, our community considers exclusivity as something to be bestowed on those deserving of it," said Ryan. "We like to think of ourselves as a force of good, cocooned within the rotten apple that is the city."

The old man mopped his brow with a handkerchief. He licked his lips. "So it's totally self contained?"

"Absolutely. Here—you'll see." Ryan stopped the car in front of the metal gate. He ignored the keypad, instead touching a small electronic key-fob against a sensor in the pillar. There was a beep and the electric gate began to slide across, allowing them entry. He drove through and paused in front of an identical gate. The one behind them slid closed and Ryan activated the sensor on the next one. Soon they were entering the main street of Priory.

The thoroughfare was long, bordered on both sides by a row of single-storey houses. They all looked identical in design. Unassuming. Comfortable.

There was a post box on the left. The car crawled along the road as the old man wriggled nervously. It was clear that he'd gone to some effort to impress Ryan. He was wearing a crisp cotton shirt, a bow-tie fastened at his neck. His hair was combed into a neat parting, though drops of perspiration speckled his forehead. A pair of spectacles completed the studious image. The bow-tie in particular lent the man an aura of old-fashioned refinement.

"My goodness, this is splendid."

Ryan noted the expensive cut of the man's clothes, smelt his designer cologne. "And your generous donation means we can continue to work hard in the community to spread the Lord's word."

"So I'll live, where—in one of these houses?" There was a sense of awe in the man's voice.

"Indeed."

They reached the curve of the bend and a large house loomed into view, deliberately placed at the end of the road like a statement of intent. Unlike the others on the street, this house sported a wooden veranda, two storeys, and an imposing gothic turret. It was a far grander building, constructed of stone and slate, much older than the others. Ryan heard the old man inhale beside him.

"And that," said Ryan, "is the home of our spiritual leader, Charles Erich. You'll have a chance to meet him later."

"Oh, this is all so nice."

They stopped a little way along the road, outside one of the identical bungalows. Ryan helped the old man out of the car and they strolled up the garden path. The man marvelled at the matching lawns, the neat wooden gates, the identical flowerbeds bordering white picket-fences. It was almost possible to forget the spike-topped walls and electric security gates, and instead believe you were on a normal suburban street.

As they entered the house, Ryan explained the schedule. "My wife's involved in church matters at the moment. I expect she'll be over around lunchtime to say hello. For now, I'll show you around the place—let you see how we live in harmony together." He paused for a second. "You'll come to see that our church is quite unlike those of other faiths. Most people wouldn't understand. Many other religions would oppose what we stand for, what our scriptures teach. But you'll come to learn that our way is the only way."

The man murmured his assent as Ryan conducted a quick tour of his home. He seemed to have calmed down a little; he'd even loosened his bow-tie and rolled back the sleeves of his shirt. "My goodness, these houses are more spacious than they look." He glanced at a photo frame on the bookcase. "That your son? What a lovely family you have."

"Yes, that's him sitting on my wife's knee. He's a good lad."

For a moment the old man seemed to struggle to get his emotion under control. He looked Ryan directly in the eye. "This is why it would mean so much—to live at Priory, I mean." He mopped his brow. "For the past few years I've been lost. At the end of my tether, nothing much to live for. Meeting you at the hotel that day was a sign. I believe the Lord reached out a hand to me."

"He did indeed."

"I know my financial donation will go to good use, but it's the community I'm most looking forward to being a part of. For so long my life has had no purpose. Now I know where I belong." He gripped Ryan's forearm. "Thank you so much for letting me come."

Ryan smiled. "It's Mr Erich you should be thanking. He's our director, the head of our church."

The old man nodded. "I'll be sure to thank him, too. Where is the church, by the way?"

"C'mon, I'll show you something quite clever." Ryan led the man through to the study at the back of the house. There was a wooden trapdoor in the corner. "Our church is carved out of the ground. There's a series of tunnels beneath the house that are all joined. That way we can come and go without the prying eyes of the public."

The man's eyes gleamed. He glanced around the study. There was a painting on the wall which caught his attention. "Wow—that's beautiful."

They both moved so they were standing in front of the painting, which depicted a storm raging at sea, as a half-submerged creature reached skyward from between a series of mountainous waves.

"Imaginative and powerful." He studied it for a moment. Then he drew out of his pocket a sheet of yellow paper and unfolded it. It was one of the flyers that Ryan distributed. "It's the same," he said, pointing to the symbol in the corner. "And I noticed it in the pattern on the gates at the entrance. I thought it was an octopus, but it's not really, is it?"

"No, it's not," said Ryan quietly. "It's a mythical creature—one upon which our religion is based. A symbol of what we stand for." There was a series of shelves lining the back wall, cluttered with objects. Ryan moved some books to one side and revealed a huge jar. He lifted it down and held it so the old man could see.

"My goodness, what's that?" The man gaped at the creature floating in the liquid. It was a grotesque tentacled mass with a huge circular eye and a ribbed, beak-like mouth. Its skin looked unpleasantly pale.

"This is what the religion is based on," said Ryan. "Or at least one of the things."

"Looks like a deformed squid. Or a cuttlefish."

"It's strange, isn't it? There's a curious legend attached to it. In the late 1880s a clergyman was out walking on the beach when he stumbled across the flotsam and jetsam from a schooner that had been brought down in a storm. He searched through the debris for a while until he came across this odd little creature wriggling on the sand. The clergyman was also knowledgeable in the science of natural history, yet he failed to recognise what the creature was. And as he leaned in close to examine it he heard voices coming from what he assumed to be its mouth. Actual words. And so the story goes that he cocked his ear to the creature and listened to what it had to say."

The old man's mouth was agape.

Ryan continued, enjoying the effect his storytelling

skills were having on the man. "The clergyman took the creature home with him. He feasted on knowledge and understanding, the likes of which had previously been beyond man's limit of comprehension. He gave up his religion and formed a new one, based on the teachings of this creature. He was bestowed with great insight into the dealings of gods—ancient and supremely powerful—which combined to form a quartet that comprise the four corners of our faith. According to legend, they were the offspring of such a primeval creature.

"One of the siblings was feathered—born of the air. One was made of sand and rock; the third—of ash and flame. And this beauty—our Lord's first son—was stolen from the sea."

The old man examined the strange creature with a mixture and awe and revulsion. Ryan fancied he was holding his breath in an effort to hear if the animal was speaking to him through the glass of the jar. His eyes had a dazed look, like he was imagining the possibility of spending the rest of his life here.

Ryan knew he'd nailed it.

"Once again I'd like to thank you for your interest in our church," said Ryan. He bowed his head. "It's only through the generosity of dedicated people like yourself that enables us to do things like this—go out into the community and spread the good word."

The old woman clutched the pamphlets to her chest and pumped his hand vigorously. "Well I don't have much but I'm sure it'll come to some use. Like I said, I'd be very happy to put my bungalow on the market and move in to those beautiful homes you talked about."

"I'm sure you'll fit right in." He had to eventually extricate his hand from hers. "Priory is quite unlike anywhere else."

They were in the foyer of the Royal Hotel. Its plush elegance supported the image that Ryan was keen to promote. Leafy palms were strategically placed in an effort to create a relaxed environment.

The woman hesitated for a moment. "There's just one thing I wanted to ask . . . "

"Of course?"

"It's just that I have a little Yorkshire terrier—Mitzi—and I really don't think I'd be able to leave her behind . . . "

Ryan flashed his winning smile. "Let's wait for the donation to clear, then we'll meet as arranged and let you have a look around Priory." He winked at her and said conspiratorially, "Mitzi's going to love it there."

She beamed in response and studied the pamphlet for a second. Just then Ryan's phone started ringing. He glanced at the display, and frowned.

"I'm sorry—I'll just have to take this."

"Of course . . . "

He pressed the button. "Hi, love. How are you?"

"Ryan—you need to come home."

"Caitlin, what is it? Your voice sounds-"

"It's Benjamin—there's been an accident."

"Accident? What do you mean-"

"He's been knocked down, Ryan. You need to come home now."

He heard a loud rushing sound in his ears. Beside him the old woman's concern faded into a meaningless mumble. His vision flickered, a wave of dizziness surged through his head. Darkness claimed him.

The rain drummed on the roof of the bus-shelter like a faltering pulse, sporadic and random. Ryan could almost imagine the drops were a message beat out in Morse code, the meaning of which was unknown. Every one of his senses felt numb. Detached. He watched the drips running down the Perspex side, distorting his view of the town beyond. Sometimes it was hard to tell if he was still crying.

Cars swept by like watery ghosts. He seemed only to notice them once they'd gone, the only evidence of their passing a swish of wheels on the tarmac, the tremble of puddles in their wake. It made him feel sedentary.

He had been here for nearly an hour, huddled inside his coat. Buses had come and gone, passengers had queued and boarded; some had disembarked and hurried away to their homes or places of work. The restless movement reminded him that lives were being lived somewhere.

From the bus shelter he could see Priory's perimeter wall, an inconspicuous barrier of ochre bricks that ran the length of the road opposite. He blinked, wondering whether the wall was in actual fact to keep people out, or contain something within. For many years he had considered it home. Now it was just a place filled with silence and cruel memories.

He was meant to be attending to some paperwork but the thought of sitting at his desk, inside the claustrophobic house, left him gasping. He had sought the reassurance that life existed beyond the borders of Priory, that there was more to the world than the confines of his faith.

Not for the first time he had the feeling that he was being watched. His eyes scanned the drivers of the passing cars, the faces of the people hurrying by—all of them unrecognisable. Yet the feeling that he was being observed persisted.

Just then his mobile phone vibrated. He glanced at the screen and in an instant he felt a shifting in the clouds above as sunlight brightened the street momentarily. The caller display had the cryptic attribute *N* showing. He answered the phone, noticing how the tone of his voice had been altered by the sudden smile that had transformed it.

The day before Ben's cremation, Ryan had visited his son's body at the funeral parlour. He could recall nothing at all now about the twenty five minutes he'd spent there, other than at some point he'd washed his hands in the bathroom at the back of the building. Since then the smell of carbolic soap had clung to him like a haze.

Ryan's job involved him travelling a fair bit. On the days when he was away he could almost forget about his usual life and instead fantasise that he was a normal man out on the road, a salesman maybe or a rep, moving from motel to motel. The smell of carbolic soap was still there, but it lingered low in his consciousness.

Ryan dreaded returning home. It felt like the old stone building was also bereft of Ben, whose absence had been filled with silence and the ticking of structural beams, the hiss of ancient radiators. Sometimes when Ryan was alone he heard floorboards creak in the study next door. He tried not to think about its cause, preferring to ignore the sounds and focus on preventing his whole life from disintegrating. Caitlin spent a great deal of her time at the house at the end of the street, conversing with Charles Erich. She'd often return hours later, her eyes blazing with fervour, her faith reinvigorated. When he wasn't on the road he'd sometimes feel jealous that he wasn't permitted to attend these meetings, to which only the church Elders were invited. Lately however this arrangement had suited Ryan. When Caitlin was at home the atmosphere felt coiled and tense. At the weekends he'd spend hours in the living room, staring at stationary dust motes trapped in the shafts of light pouring through the window. They were reminders of how immobile the house had become, how motionless their life now was. They were no longer a married couple; they were just exhibits in a specimen jar. He listened to the radiators sigh their eulogies.

One morning he ventured to the rear of the house. Ben's door had remained closed since his death. Ryan had not been able to face going in. He gripped the doorknob and breathed deep. It felt like a test he was too frightened to take. He turned and walked back along the corridor. The study door was also closed.

Since Ben's death it had been taken over by Caitlin. Often he'd hear her in the room, muttering scripture, her voice almost unrecognisable. She had changed so much herself; it was like Ben's loss had taken something of her away with him.

At that moment he heard her enter through the front door. He ran his hand across his hair to flatten it, and hurried into the hallway. She had deposited some books on the table by the phone.

"Hi."

She smiled wanly. "Just been to morning service." He noticed she was wearing that dress she had worn at the summer fair the previous year. She stopped abruptly, peering at him. "What's wrong? You look . . . strange."

He rubbed his grizzled chin. "Caitlin . . . I . . . we need to talk."

"Yes, of course, darling," she said, walking business-like through into the living room. He followed her absently. She waved him into a chair, but remained standing herself, glancing down at him. "What is it? Are you ill?"

Ryan combed his fingers through his hair, and shrugged, distracted. "I'm struggling . . . With Ben."

He couldn't be sure but he thought he detected a faint tone of impatience in her manner. She looked at him directly. "That's understandable. It's only been eight months. I'm only just getting over it myself." She offered a smile that looked heavily compensated. "But we have to stay strong. Remember—it's the Lord's will. We're not here to question, we're here to pledge our faith to the Lord. It's only our struggles in this world that will enable us to—"

"Listen, there's another thing—I don't know how much longer I can go on pretending like this."

"What's that supposed to mean?"

"To the church. I can't keep up this fake bravado." He exhaled. "I'm hurting, Caitlin, and I'm finding it hard to understand how people as . . . committed to the faith as we are can be going through such pain. Doesn't it make you question what kind of a god allows an innocent boy to die, and turn a blind eye to other things that go on?"

Her cheeks were red as if she'd been slapped. "Ryan, I thought we were both committed members of this church. I thought we shared the highs and lows together. I thought we both understood that death does not mean the end."

"We do." He closed his eyes and rubbed his face with his hands. "But . . . I'm sorry, I think I'm just feeling a bit . . . *isolated* at the moment."

She sat down next to him and rubbed his shoulder. It felt like the way you'd pet a dog. "It's okay, it's okay. Listen, tell you what—I'll have a word with Charles; see if I can get you off the road for a while. The Elders will understand. See if it'll help having you closer to home, here at the church."

He felt suddenly alarmed, like he was being trapped. He swallowed and made a concerted effort to look at her. "Honestly, I'll be fine. Sometimes it catches up with you, you know?"

"Of course." She stood and smoothed down the dress. "Now let's hear no more negativity. Benjamin's in a better place now. The accident was dealt with, so let's put it behind us."

He watched her as she left the room, her perfume's aroma quickly dampened by the smell of carbolic soap.

They usually met at a quiet bar in town. There was always a corner booth available where they could relax without the fear of being seen. Not that they had anything to hide, of course, but people were wont to talk and Ryan was keen to avoid uncomfortable questions from the Elders, or attract gossip from disapproving members of their community. At first their meetings had consisted of nothing more than mild flirting—Ryan's automatic response to interest from attractive women. He understood that his good looks drew attention from the opposite sex but he'd never taken advantage of this, instead simply utilising it as a skill in his recruitment efforts. Besides, his faith meant that adultery was out of the question; it was simply a temptation that must not be considered. So Natalie had remained merely a friend, albeit one to whom he greatly looked forward to seeing. The clandestine aspect of it only increased the thrill.

But Ben's death had changed all that. In the aftermath of the accident their relationship had undergone a transformation. As well as his son's life, that car had torn down the pretence that had existed between them. His grief had exposed *emotion*—real emotion, not the polite façade that they'd perpetuated before. Natalie's role in his life became so much more vital. In the immediate weeks following Ben's death, Ryan took solace in Natalie's balanced sympathy. She gave him room to deal with the loss, something that was not permitted at home. He was left feeling brittle and detached by his wife's assertion that their overriding faith would guide them. He found himself drawn to Natalie, suddenly realising that his feelings were gathering pace.

As the season changed and the days grew warmer he began to dread the approaching summer, which would herald painful reminders—memories of playing in the park, days on the beach, a time once filled with hope and optimism.

By the end of February Ryan was feeling fragile and exposed. And it was then, when he was at his most vulnerable, that Natalie suggested they run away together.

They were in their usual booth. The only other patrons were two overweight pensioners perched on stools at the bar. Barely audible music seeped from a speaker positioned above the pinball machine. Out on the street, vague figures occasionally wandered past. Ryan's heart was in his mouth. He watched the pensioners at the bar, trying to read their lips. The barman was busy restocking his refrigerators with beer. The sporadic chink of bottles was hypnotic. Ryan felt like he was drifting in and out of a dream. He reached out and took Natalie's hand.

He blinked several times as he considered her words. "What do you mean?"

"We could just move away, where no one knows us. Start a new life. Forget about what's happened." Her dark eyes blazed with conviction. He could see the possibility in her face.

"What about Caitlin?" he said slowly. He could feel his chest tightening.

Natalie exhaled, her eyes wide. "What about *us*?"

He pursed his lips and took a sip of his drink. He thought about the stories he'd heard; what had happened to previous members of the church who'd lost their faith. He swallowed. The two old guys at the bar were too far away to hear. They weren't even looking his way. From somewhere out on the street a car honked its horn. It felt like an omen. He nodded.

Natalie drew his hand up and kissed the back of it. "Ry, you've said this yourself—there's nothing for you here now. Your wife's too wrapped up in herself to care what you do." She brushed her cheek against his fingers. "You know how I feel about you. We could start a new life together."

He laughed hollowly. "What about my job?"

She looked incredulous for a second. "What about it? You can get another. You hate it anyway."

He took another drink. It was true, though he hadn't always hated it. But since Ben's death, all bets were off. Things had changed irrevocably. He had to face the fact that he and Natalie were now involved in something far more than friendship; their feelings had blossomed into something that had given his life meaning once again. "Where could we go?" His voice was quiet.

Natalie shrugged. "Well, my uncle has a house in the north-west, up near the coast. He's had to move into a nursing home." She looked him directly in the eye. "He's not expected to come out. We could hole up there for a while, just till we sort things out."

Ryan felt something unfurling in his chest. He was giddy. A sensation of euphoria, so intense he felt sick. He glanced up at the two old guys and the barman; all three were chatting together, not remotely interested in anything else. He nodded hesitantly.

Natalie smiled. "There'll be plenty of jobs in the summer, once the season starts up. We can start over, just the two of us. I'll give notice to my landlord. We'll throw some clothes in your car and just drive north. Leave everything behind."

"I'm due out on the road again next week." He chewed his lip, stared at the surface of his drink. "We could go then. It'd be four days before I was missed. By then we could be miles away."

"Yes." She leaned forward to kiss him. "It's time to think about us now."

When Caitlin began to speak, Ryan had no idea how long he'd been staring at the half-written letter in front of him. He glanced up at her, confusion wrinkling his brow. "Sorry?"

"I said it's time you sorted yourself out." His wife's voice was clipped and unsympathetic. "Wallowing in self-pity will do you no good."

He was in the living-room, working on some church letters that needing sending out. He hadn't even heard Caitlin returning home. Her sudden appearance felt like a violation of the silence in which he'd been engrossed.

"Cait, I'm just . . . working, that's all."

She raised an eyebrow. "You were staring into space." She came into the living room and sat in the armchair opposite. Ryan blew out his cheeks and leaned back in the sofa. He put his fountain pen down on the coffee-table.

"The thing is," she said, "Charles has asked me to speak to you . . . "

"What about?"

She shrugged. "Well—your figures for one thing."

"What's wrong with my figures? The last report I filed showed a big increase on this time last year—up by nearly fifteen percent." He ran his fingers through his hair.

"Not just the financial income, Ryan—it's more the lack of *physical investment*."

He began counting things off on his fingers. "But there was the elderly couple last month, that widower and her disabled son, that homeless lad with the drug problem. And that's just since February."

"Mr Erich thinks your mind is elsewhere." She moved so she was sitting beside him. "You don't seem to have the same focus you once had." She patted his knee. It felt like a parody of affection. "You've changed."

He swallowed. "Cait, we've both been through so much, I'm not sure I feel the same anymore."

"I knew it." She nodded firmly.

"What I mean is—my heart isn't in it like it used to be." He could feel his chin trembling under the weight of emotion that was threatening to spill. "Losing Ben has been tough."

"Of course it has-"

"And it's made me question whether I want to put my faith in a god that allows such a thing to happen." He glared at her defiantly, waiting for her explosion.

The only sign was a slight narrowing of her eyes. "Ryan, how dare you question the Lord? I never thought I'd see the day when you'd become such a blasphemer."

"Well don't you think it's bizarre? When we were invested into this church we were told that only good would come to us; that all our wishes would be granted, that if we showed faith we'd be rewarded. How has our son dying benefited us?" He laughed incredulously. "What kind of god allows an innocent child to die like that?"

Her voice was measured, controlled. "Life's a test, you know that. The daily struggles we endure are just obstacles that we must overcome if we're to be rewarded in the next life."

"What about *this* life? What if we're wasting our time doing aimless things that mean nothing in the end?" He hitched a sob. "I can't come to terms with what happened to Ben. He was in hospital and everyone prayed and prayed, and what use did it do?"

"Ryan, you need to listen to me, and you need to listen good—this attitude is doing you a great deal of damage. You need to snap out of it." She stood up and picked an invisible piece of thread off her sleeve. "Mr Erich has warned me that unless things improve, action will have to be taken." She turned and breezed out of the room.

Ryan closed his eyes, but not before he was able to prevent the tears from coming.

The farther away from the town he was, the less trapped he felt. It wasn't just the accident that had changed Ryan's perspective—what hurt was the casual way he seemed to have been marginalised by their church. He thought about the hierarchy of the religious community, and it rankled to see the different levels. Sometimes his wife's enthusiasm for their faith infuriated him.

"This feels great," said Natalie, snapping him out of his reverie.

He turned to her, blinking. They were in the car, trundling out into the countryside. He'd picked her up on the outskirts of town, daring to pull up in the loading bay of the museum, from whose doorway she'd darted, and slipped into the passenger seat.

"Being here with you, I mean." She smiled at him.

He returned the gesture. When he was in Natalie's company he felt like he could be himself, rather than a messenger for their Lord, a servant for their church. When he thought of how strong his faith once was, it seemed jarring to now feel so much contempt.

They talked about the things that mattered to them—the house belonging to Natalie's uncle, how nice it would be to live on the coastline for the summer, how much they were looking to being together. But there were unspoken things lying in the back of Ryan's mind that he didn't want to deal with— the impact of leaving his wife, the effect of running out on the church, even an absurd fear that he was being selfish in the aftermath of his son's death.

Natalie had explained that she'd withdrawn a large sum of cash from the bank. Each small step like this felt like it was becoming more real, and it made Ryan giddy. He told her there was a large quantity of cash in the house and he'd take it on the day they made the break. It should certainly keep them going for quite a while.

"Do you think she'll try to find you?" Natalie asked.

For ages he didn't speak, just stared ahead through the windscreen. Then he pursed his lips. "I think my employers will be more bothered. I expect they'll look for me." He didn't voice the real concerns he harboured—those stories he'd heard about past members of the church who had previously managed to flee. He'd started to believe that the whispered rumours of execution and physical punishment might hold an element of truth.

"What's it to do with them? It's your life."

He laughed hollowly. "Unfortunately they don't view it that way."

She looked thoughtful for a minute. "I hope you don't mind me saying this . . . "

"Go on."

"Well—I totally respect your right to worship, and all that . . . "

"But?"

"Well, it just seems a bit . . . *unorthodox*." She added quickly, "Not that there's anything wrong with that, of course, but-"

He took a deep breath. "It *is* an unconventional church, but none more so than any other. It's just that ours has a smaller congregation." He looked at her. There was so much that he couldn't possibly talk about.

"Having a hidden church is *definitely* unconventional."

"Look, I've told you before—it's not hidden, it's just constructed so that the chambers of worship are below the street."

"So it's hidden."

"Not hidden, no." He paused while the car pulled out of a junction onto the main road. They were on the dual carriageway that led out of town. He had been glancing at the drivers of cars that passed, seeing if he recognised any of them. The vigilance was beginning to tire him. "Admittedly some of the iconography is a bit weird. Not conventional."

He saw her nod, could detect the regret in her face. They were here to spend time in each others' company, were on the brink of running away together. Not argue—although technically they weren't even approaching the point of arguing—it was more of an uncomfortable discussion. And the whole point was *discomfort* was precisely what he'd begun to feel.

She spoke as if she'd read his thoughts. "It bothers you, doesn't it—this weird religion?"

He shrugged. "I suppose it was Caitlin that drove us to it. She was always the devout one, always the one with the unwavering belief. I think it had something to do with her upbringing."

"And you weren't as sure?"

He shrugged again, uncertainty moulding his face into a mask. "I *was* once, but since Ben . . . well, what I mean is, it shifts your thinking a bit."

Natalie laid a gentle hand on his leg. "I know, Ry. I know."

They were driving up into the hills. Green fields flew past, sheep grazed in meadows, hedgerows crowded their view.

After a while he continued speaking. "Listen, I feel bad for saying this, 'cause after Ben's accident we both prayed. Prayed like our own lives depended on it. And the Elders were there for us. I just felt so helpless, so . . .

unable to do anything . . . I've never felt like that before." He blinked rapidly and a few tears spilled onto his cheek. His voice held firm, but it was hushed, barely audible. "Caitlin insisted that the accident was the Lord's will. I was just angry. Numb. I was raging inside. I prayed for revenge."

Natalie stroked his forearm. "You were upset, that's all. It's nothing to feel guilty about-"

"The driver of the car was a young woman. She hadn't been drinking or anything. It was just an accident. And that made it all the more devastating. There was no one to blame." He brushed the tears from his face. "A month after it happened, she was found dead in her home. They think she'd killed herself. Her windpipe was blocked with rocks and gravel."

"Gravel?"

"Well—shale, soil. She'd choked on it. They think she might not have been a full shilling. Of course Caitlin took that as a sign of our faithfulness, like it was a reward for our prayers." He neglected to give voice to his suspicions; that the church had meted out their own method of revenge.

Natalie almost laughed, but stopped herself. It was absurd, so finely balanced. She was mindful of his beliefs—despite the fact that its foundations were beginning to show signs of crumbling—and tried to be respectful, so she said nothing.

They stopped at a parking area on the peak of a hill. They could see for miles. Despite the isolation, Ryan scanned the horizon for signs of watching figures, only relaxing when he was confident they were alone. The late spring sunshine was warm, its brightness accentuating the blue sky, the green grass, creating a stark contrast between his dark stuffy house and the open space of the countryside. They took a blanket from the car and walked until they found a suitable spot beneath the shade of a towering oak tree. They chatted some more, but this time it was different. They did not discuss their past, instead preferring to laugh and joke and do their best to repair the disquiet that they'd stirred between them.

"Tell me about your uncle's house," he said. He lay with his head on her knee and she stroked his hair.

"It's an old rambling fisherman's cottage on the edge of a cliff. There's a track that's overgrown with flowers and bushes, and it leads down to the beach. In the summer the smell of lavender is so strong. We could get a little dog—a Jack Russell or a Cairn terrier—and we could walk it along the beach, listening to the seagulls and watching the tide. In the summer the sun will sparkle on the sea and we'll sit on the dunes and read or have a picnic like this. At night we'll eat at the pub at the crossroads or I'll cook, and we could make love in the bed, with the window open, listening to the sounds of the sea crashing on the shore."

The bag of clothes was waiting for him in the hallway.

"Do you mind taking them to the furnace?" asked Caitlin, slipping on her suit jacket. "I have an afternoon service to prepare for."

Ryan nodded. He was finishing his toast, waiting

for the moment when she would leave for work and the welcoming silence would arrive.

She continued her power-strides around the house for another few minutes before calling out a perfunctory *goodbye* and exiting. The slam of the door, followed by her fading heels on the concrete, acted as a pacifier to his mood.

Once he'd finished his breakfast and washed up the dishes he walked into the hallway and examined the bag. It contained a large collared shirt and a pair of polyester trousers (both men's), a floral blouse and a pleated skirt. At the bottom was a pair of women's court shoes and two scuffed brown brogues. The clothes smelled vaguely stale, like the interior of a caravan or a charity shop. He ran his fingers over the silk blouse, enjoying the softness and the cut of the material.

He picked up the bag and left the house. The street was deserted. There was a service building over in the corner of the cul-de-sac and he paused outside a door set into a recessed arch. He punched four numbers into its keypad and the door clicked open. He entered the service building and stood for a moment in the foyer, listening to the low rumble of the machinery, feeling a faint vibration coming up through his feet. There was a series of doors to his right but he ignored them and walked through the one to his left, descending a narrow flight of stairs. Opening the door had triggered a set of automatic lights, and they flickered on ahead of him as he made his way into the basement.

The noise was much louder down here. Gears and cogs ground together behind the walls. A faint glow emanated from a series of holes punched into a metal sheet measuring six feet square. There was a handle in its centre. He raised it, revealing a stationary conveyor belt. Its metal rollers were tightly built. He lifted the clothes out of the bag and placed them on the conveyor belt. Just as he was doing the same with the shoes he noticed that there were a few objects inside one of them. It was a pair of false teeth and a hearing-aid. He looked at them for a moment before returning them to the court shoe and placing them on the conveyor belt. The brogue also contained something extra; a pair of spectacles and a spotted bowtie. He studied the bowtie for a while, thinking about its simple beauty and how in a few minutes it would be lost forever.

He placed all the items on the conveyor belt and pressed a button set into the metal body of the incinerator. There was a short pause then the conveyor belt whirred into life and began to transport the clothing towards the rear of the incinerator. He bent to watch its progress. Once it was about eight or nine feet in, just a short distance from the back of the furnace, the conveyor belt reached its end and plummeted its cargo into the fire. An orange flickering bloomed against the metal interior.

The conveyor belt returned to its stationary position. For a while he contemplated the bow tie, how one minute he was able to touch it and appreciate its beauty, its simplistic appeal that he could all too easily take for granted—and how, within a short space of time, it no longer existed as anything other than smoke and ash, just a mere memory.

He rubbed at his eyes and slowly trudged upstairs.

Ryan watched the street. The net curtains of their bedroom offered him a protective cloak, a veil of invisibility. As usual there wasn't a great deal of movement. At one point he spotted the geologist's wife from further up the street appear at her window, all pale-faced and furrowed brow. In the days immediately following Ben's death he'd considered approaching her. The awkward alienation she displayed seemed to speak to him in a way that was otherwise absent in others. But the moment had passed and he subsequently found sanctuary in Natalie. Now Ryan watched her melancholy movement with a deep sense of regret. She stroked her cat for a few minutes as it arched its back on the sill, and the gesture of affection almost moved Ryan to tears.

At exactly ten-thirty he saw Charles Erich, the gaunt leader of their church, appear at the window of his own house and draw the curtains. Ryan could see figures standing behind him but was unable to spot whether one of them was Caitlin, although he noticed the Elder called Mr Philips there.

He walked to the study and tried the door but it was locked. His bag was in the hall. He removed a personal organiser from the zippered pocket and slid out the small duplicate key that he'd had cut at the cobbler's in Exham. He returned to the study and unlocked the door.

The air was stale, mildly unpleasant. It had been

months since he'd been in the here, yet it seemed like nothing at all had been moved despite the hours that Caitlin spent in it. He peered at the jar on the shelf for a moment, watching the languid movement of the creature as it drifted in the liquid. Its saucer eye appeared to regard him, no matter where he stood in the room.

A low rumbling emanated from the trapdoor. Ryan moved over to it and knelt, pressing his ear to the wood. He could hear a distant noise—the gasping of pistons, a grind of machinery; the vague metallic squeal of gears. The trapdoor vibrated faintly against his cheek. Somehow Ryan felt afraid. There was a deep timbre to the sound that made him feel insignificant. Powerless.

He sat up and turned to glance at the thing in the jar, which just stared back at him through the dust-coated glass, now yellowed with age.

Ryan stood and hurried out of the study, locking the door behind him, trying to quell the notion that the sound of the squealing gears held any semblance of a human voice.

As soon as he emerged from the bank he felt the wind whipping at his clothing, ruffling his hair. He caught a glimpse of his reflection in the smoked glass, noticing his hollow eyes, the grizzled chin, the sallow complexion of his face—he looked like a man who was up to no good.

The pedestrian precinct was busy at this hour of

the morning. He double-checked the cash he'd withdrawn from the bank was safely stowed in the inside pocket of his jacket, then set off walking towards the car park. He had only gone a few steps when a voice spoke from his right. "Excuse me, mister."

He turned to see a pale woman wearing jeans and a hooded top peering at him. She looked to be in her early thirties. Beside her, a young boy clutched her hand so tightly it was like the wind threatened to snatch him away. "We were wondering if you'd have room for us?"

"What?" Ryan blinked, trying to reset the track of his thought process.

"We came to one of your seminars last year," the woman explained. "Me and my husband. Only at the time it weren't right for us." She glanced down at her son. "But he's walked out on us and . . . well, now it seems like the right time."

Ryan turned and peered across to where his car was parked. The bulge of cash in his pocket felt conspicuous. "Oh—right."

"You were at the Pavilion Hotel last June?" she prompted. "We donated something to your church but we weren't able to visit." The wind flicked her hair into a tangle, which she drew away from her face. "But now Alan's gone and I'm behind with the rent. If we could stay at Priory I can give notice to the landlord. I've only got the car but it's up for sale and I should get fifteen-hundred easy." The signs of desperation were visible in her face. Even the boy peered up at him with an imploring look.

"I'm sorry," said Ryan. "I . . . I don't work for the church any more."

"Oh?" For a moment she looked confused. "Only the man at the Pavilion said you'd done another seminar there a few weeks ago."

He looked down at the boy. He seemed about 7 or 8. He was wearing an *Adventure Time* T-shirt, similar to the one his son once owned. Those dark eyes were like a knife in Ryan's chest. He could detect the aroma of carbolic soap in his nostrils.

"I'm sorry," he said at last. "I don't think I can help." He began to push past her, hurrying through the crowd of shoppers.

"Wait!" She hastened after him, barging into a couple of pedestrians. "Please help us. We've nowhere else to go." She grabbed the sleeve of his jacket.

He stopped and turned abruptly. He leaned in close. "Listen, I don't do that anymore. Believe me—coming to Priory's the last thing you want to do." He had a sudden thought. He reached inside his jacket and removed the wad of cash. He unfolded three or four notes and pressed them into her hand. "Do yourself a favour and stay away from that church. This should keep you going for a while—till you're back on your feet."

He hurried away from her, through the crowd towards his car, the woman's protests ringing in his ears.

For a few agonising moments Ryan thought she wasn't there, and a chill crept into his stomach, but then he spotted her move from the shelter of a tree and begin hurrying towards his car. Relief drew a deep breath from him. She was wheeling a suitcase, beaming at him a little hesitantly as she approached. She seemed oblivious to the falling rain. He climbed out and helped her load the suitcase into the back of his car. She kissed him, pressed her body against his like she hadn't seen him in ages.

He drew back and glanced around instinctively. She laughed and said, "We don't need to worry about being seen any more."

"I suppose not." He shrugged.

"C'mon. I can't wait to get away from this place."

They climbed into the car and Ryan set off. It was mid-morning; the roads were light with traffic. Soon they were reaching the town limits. The screech of the windscreen wipers grated on his nerves. Despite Natalie's excited chitchat and reassuring manner, Ryan felt nervous as the car idled at a set of traffic lights. Perhaps it was the clandestine way they were making their escape, or had the enormity of what he was doing just registered? He swallowed and glanced in the rear-view mirror at the car behind him, but the driver's face was unfamiliar. He tried to calm himself down.

"You okay?"

He turned to Natalie. "Yeah, just a bit jumpy that's all."

She smiled and rubbed the back of his hand that rested on the gear-stick. "Don't worry. We'll wake up together tomorrow and it'll be a fresh start."

He returned the smile, more for her sake than his. "I know. I'm being silly." The lights changed and the queue of traffic began to move. "Tell me again about your uncle's cottage . . . "

She started to speak, to tell the usual patter. The fantasy that had fuelled this adventure they were about to embark on. He already had a clear idea in his mind of what it would be like. He allowed her words to soothe away his concerns.

They drove like that for a few minutes, Ryan silent, listening to Natalie indulge them in her narration. They were almost at the road heading up into the hills when he exclaimed and banged the steering wheel in annoyance.

"What's wrong?" Natalie looked anxious.

He blew out through his teeth in frustration. "I don't remember picking up the money." He clicked the indicator and pulled over.

"It doesn't matter," she said quickly. "We'll find a bank farther north."

"That's no good," he said. "There's a limit to how much I can withdraw in one day." He turned and began hunting around in the overnight bag on the back seat.

"Look, I've got money. Let's just forget about it and—"

"It's not that, Natalie, it's just that I've been squirreling it away for the past few weeks, building it up here and there so we'll have enough to live on for a while. There's quite a tidy sum. As soon as they realise I've done a runner, Caitlin will freeze the account—stop me taking any more out." What remained unsaid was that if he withdrew anything from the bank from here on in, the church would trace their movement and location—an idea that filled him with terror.

"What should we do then?"

There was nothing in the bag. He knew it. He'd left

it locked up in the drawer of his bureau at home. "We'll have to go back."

She looked concerned. "Have we got time?"

He glanced at the clock on the dashboard. "Caitlin'll be in her church duties till lunchtime. I reckon it'll take us no longer than twenty minutes to drive back. I'll just nip in and grab the cash."

She nodded. "Okay then."

He spun the car round in the road and headed back the way they had come. Maybe that's why he'd felt nervous—his subconscious mind trying to warn him he'd forgotten something? This did little to ease the anxiety.

They drove in silence. Ryan threw occasional glances at Natalie out of the corner of his eye. She chewed her lower lip and stared ahead. A faint frown had creased her brow. He negotiated the streets, concentrating on the job at hand, mentally cursing himself for his forgetfulness. Soon the chimneys of Priory became visible above the roofs of the surrounding houses. Natalie looked nervous in the passenger seat. "Want me to wait for you here while you nip in?"

Ryan pursed his lips. "No, just duck down. I'll cover you with my coat. I'll be in and out of the house in a sec."

She nodded and shuffled down in her seat, trying to curl into a ball. Ryan took his coat off the back and draped it over her. To anyone casually peering into the car it would just look like a bundle on the passenger seat. He drove up to the gates and used his electronic fob to gain access to the inner courtyard; then a quick swipe allowed him to drive through so he was inside the walls of Priory.

"I'll just nip in and out," he muttered to the still bundle next to him. He drew up outside his house. There was not a single sign of life. From here he could see Erich's imposing house at the head of the street, also silent. He climbed out of the car and walked up his drive, whistling nonchalantly as if he hadn't a care in the world. He had to concentrate to avoid hurrying in an obvious way.

As soon as he stepped inside the house his movement quickened. He dashed into the living room and unlocked the bureau's drawer. There was a manila envelope hidden beneath the mounds of insurance policies, bank statements and other documents that contained the cash. He rolled the notes up and stuffed them into his pocket, then went out into the hallway.

The enormity of the moment suddenly dawned on him. He threw a glance along the passage to the closed door of his son's room. In a moment he was about to escape the life he'd lived for the past decade a life of commitment to their church, the balancing act of being a father and a husband, the recent slow erosion of his personality as his wife's fanaticism filled the void that had been caused by his son's death. Ryan realised that the only photograph he had of Ben was a dog-eared baby picture tucked inside his wallet. That wasn't enough to last him the rest of his life.

He went to his son's room and pushed open the door. Memories collided with emotion as he viewed the room, smelt the gentle aroma of familiarity. An odour of soap hovered somewhere in Ryan's head, but the talcum powder bunny, the plastic pretend food, the oily tang of his son's train set, won the overriding battle. He stepped inside. His son's old dressing-gown still hung from the corner of his bed, its belt draping across the carpet like a snake. There was a photograph on the chest of drawers—a laughing Ben staring down from the highest point of a see-saw, taken just months before his death—and Ryan picked it up and stared at it. He knew he should go; but the idea of leaving things like this behind arrested his movement. Instead he twisted the back of the frame and slid out the photo, tucking it into his pocket. Then he froze.

Someone was coming in through the front door. He heard it close, then the clatter of footsteps on the hall tiles. He held his breath. Someone was tiptoeing along the passage. He glanced around, frantic, his heart pounding. In an instant he felt things being snatched away, their new life, his plans, the escape from his miserable existence. Suddenly a pale-faced Natalie appeared at the door. "Is everything okay?"

"My god, you scared me to death!" Relief cracked a grin to his face, but his tone was sharp. "I said I'd only be a minute."

She frowned, looked confused. "I thought you beckoned me in?"

"When?"

"Just then. Through the front window?"

"No," he said slowly. "I wasn't at the window."

The sound of the door opening again, Natalie's head turning as she peered along the passage—both these things happened simultaneously. Ryan's heart leapt. His legs nearly buckled.

"Well, well, well—what have we here?" It was Caitlin's voice from the hallway, clipped and steely.

Ryan rushed to the door, brushed Natalie to one side. Caitlin stood smiling at him from the hallway.

The emaciated figure of Charles Erich was behind her, limned by the sunlight pouring in through the window of the front door. Mr Philips stood at his side.

"I always knew you were weak," said Caitlin. "That you were not up to the job."

Ryan glanced around, panicked. He threw a glance at the closed door of the study. It looked impassive. He ducked back into his son's room, dragging Natalie with him, who yelped in surprise. He slammed the door shut.

"Pass me that!" He pressed his foot against the base of the door, and motioned to the wooden chair under the desk.

She handed it to him and he angled its position so that the back was tucked under the door handle. He paused, but there was no sound from the other side of the door; the handle remained still. He took a hesitant step back.

"What should we do?" whispered Natalie.

A shadow crossed the room and Ryan glanced at the window. Through the net curtains he could see several figures crowding against the glass—all members of the church. He yanked the curtains closed, turned his back on it. There was a spike of fear in his stomach.

Natalie clicked on the light-switch. She peered at him. "What should we do?"

He felt exposed by the brightness, blinked in confusion and fear. The door handle suddenly rattled. A volley of bangs against the wood. A splintering sound from the door jamb. He could hear murmured voices from the window, see heads trying to peer in through the closed curtains. The door handle turned with deliberate intent. Ryan tried to focus, sizing up the situation, realizing with a cold inevitability that there was absolutely nowhere to go.

He carefully took the cord off the dressing-gown. A series of thumps assailed the door. They were now throwing themselves against it, splintering the legs of the chair that acted as a barricade. Time was slipping away.

Natalie watched him, mouth open in shock, eyes wide in fear. In one swift movement he wound the cord round his fist and wrapped it around her neck, dragging her to the ground from behind. She kicked against his legs, fighting to yank the cord from her throat. A strangled scream escaped her lips. She scratched at his face and he closed his eyes to protect them, whispering into her ear as he arched his back and tightened the cord. *It's okay. It's okay. It's okay. It's okay.* In a distant part of Ryan's brain he smelled carbolic soap. But then it was overpowered by an acrid stench as the body in his stranglehold finally collapsed, voiding its bladder and bowels. There were a few more spasms, almost mechanical in their motion, and then the body became finally still.

Ryan's sight was blurred by the tears fragmenting his eyes. He realised he was still whispering into the ear. *It's okay. It's okay. It's okay.*

It's okay.

His attention was drawn to the door as the chair leg splintered and gave way, rocking back onto the rug. The door sprang open.

Caitlin and Erich were framed in the doorway, gaping at the sight that greeted them. Ryan carefully rolled the inert body off his own. It was beyond their harm now. His body would be their only outlet for revenge. His panting breath sounded deafening in the abrupt silence. He waited for something to happen.

The figure of Charles Erich slipped away, leaving him with just Caitlin's cold stare and impassive stance. He was determined not to look away, despite every ounce of fight having left his body. Caitlin's contemptuous glare chilled him to the bone. He was resigned to his punishment. He understood that he deserved it. Tears burned in his eyes but he was too numb to move, too broken by the shock of seeing his plans disintegrate. He swallowed back the sour regret.

From somewhere in the back of the house came a loud crash. Caitlin half-turned, and through the gap he could see into the study opposite. The trapdoor leaned back against the wall. A cold fear gripped Ryan. He struggled to sit up.

Something slithered up out of the trapdoor, worming its way up into the house. Caitlin's face was animated with fear and awe. She bowed her head in reverence and stepped out of the way as the monstrous thing crept across the floor towards Ryan, almost as if it could sense his presence rather than see him—a creature so ancient it bore little resemblance to anything that had ever since existed. He could see the muscular skin flexing as it inched its hungry journey between the rooms. A deep vibration echoed beneath the floor. Ryan felt rather than heard it.

In the final moments the smell of carbolic soap returned, but it was instantly overcome by a stench of stagnant water, of aluminium and cold earth, of ash and damp soil and the ageless odour of dead leaves.

PRECIOUS THINGS

V.H. LESLIE

IT WAS A long time before Petra associated her husband's strange behaviour with the house at the end of the street. She'd always accepted Bernard as being a little unconventional, over-zealous with his research, that it was easy to believe his recent eccentricities were merely another facet of his personality. Perhaps if Petra hadn't have lived with Bernard for such a long time—near on forty years—she would have recognised earlier something was seriously wrong. But it was hard to notice a decline when it occurred so gradually, each day resulting in tiny, barely seen slippages of character, like the steady erosion of a rock face.

It was even harder to pinpoint exactly *when* Bernard began to change. It could have started as early as their move to the street a few years ago, Bernard having taken early retirement. It wasn't an area Petra would have chosen, but the surrounding landscape was built on limestone and clay, which formed spectacular outcrops and countless caves, ideal for a mineralogist like Bernard. They had planned to take lots of walks; Bernard could take samples, Petra could pack a picnic. The idea appealed to her; being active was a talisman against old age. Petra had bought a pair of walking boots especially. They were still buried in the cupboard in the original shoebox.

Perhaps *that* was the first sign something was amiss. Bernard, a man who'd spent his whole career outside, now hardly ever left the house. He had been very particular about which room of their new home to make his study—it needed to be large enough to house his equipment and rock collection and to provide sufficient light for his work. It became his sanctuary, a room he very rarely left, a place forbidden to others. Perhaps that was the second sign.

Petra stood outside the door.

She'd taken to standing there a few moments before she knocked, trying to imagine what he was doing inside. What great work occupied him so entirely? As usual there was no sound at all.

Petra was careful of her ring as she balled her hand to knock on the door. Diamond. Emerald. Amethyst. Ruby. Emerald. Sapphire. Tourmaline. The stones stood out sharply above her knuckle, set in this specific order to form the acronym DEAREST.

Dearest . . .

Though it was her engagement ring, she had always suspected it was more for Bernard than for her. He loved precious things. It had been a Victorian fad, spelling out sentimental words with the initial letters of gemstones but Bernard had Petra's ring made specially, with particular stones he'd selected himself. He'd chosen tourmaline for the T, instead of topaz, which was more common. He used to polish the stones himself so they gleamed afterwards like a rainbow. Petra noticed how dull the stones had become.

She knocked again and then called through the door, "Bernard, supper's ready."

No answer. She didn't try the handle; she knew it would be locked.

She raised her hand again, glancing at her ring— *dearest*—as if it too were silently imploring her husband to answer.

"Bernard?"

There was finally movement from inside the locked room. She heard Bernard walk across the floorboards to the door.

"I'll be right out," he said.

Petra hovered outside a moment longer, feeling his fleeting presence behind the closed door, then she went to wait for him in the dining room.

Petra dished herself up some more potatoes. Bernard ate perfunctorily, as if there was no joy in it, though Petra had prepared his favourite meal. Mr Gilman curled himself around the chair leg, purring for scraps.

Petra shifted in her seat. "How's your work going, dear?"

Bernard continued eating. "Fine," he said between mouthfuls.

"It must be top secret."

Bernard didn't look up. "Just rocks."

It had always been rocks with Bernard. They'd met years ago on a stretch of Jurassic coastline. Bernard had been combing the shore, looking for fossils, when he'd discovered Petra who was holidaying with her family. He'd always maintained she was the most precious thing he had ever found.

"I've made desert," Petra said.

Bernard finished his last mouthful and placed the cutlery down.

"I think I'll have mine in the study."

Mealtimes used to be sacred. Petra had always relished these times to discuss their days, to talk about Bernard's research. But they had become more and more infrequent. Sometimes he asked her to place the food outside the door or to leave it in the oven for later. Petra thought he might as well put a hatch in the study door and she could deliver his food like a jailor.

Except the study wasn't a prison for Bernard, it was his refuge. He couldn't allow people in, he argued, because of all the hazardous tools, the delicate specimens it contained, as if the presence of others would contaminate something. But Petra knew it was because really he wanted to be on his own.

She could understand that. The rest of her house fell under her domain, feminised with floral wallpaper and chintz. There was nothing wrong with Bernard having a private space away from it all. Except that in their previous homes she'd never been denied entry, no room had ever been off limits. She missed watching Bernard work. She missed looking at his collection of minerals and the precious stones lined up in the glass cabinets. The way the clusters of crystals sparkled, the play of light in the opals, the vitreous lustre of tourmaline and spinel. But more than that she missed spending time with her husband.

"I'll leave your pudding outside," Petra said, feeding Mr Gilman from her plate surreptitiously. She managed a smile.

"Thank you," Bernard said, rising, wiping the corner of his mouth with his serviette. As he passed his wife, he touched her lightly on the shoulder and hurried back to his work.

Petra peered through the curtains at the house at the end of the street. It was pretty unassuming. A light was on in a downstairs reception room and people were sat down, unnaturally still, casting elongated shadows like stalagmite formations. Bernard was among them. Never a very social person, Bernard had begun visiting Charles Erich, the owner of the house, almost as soon as they had moved in. Petra was never invited to these soirees and when she pressed to go, Bernard insisted they would only bore her. Erich was an amateur rock collector, a fellow enthusiast of all things buried, he'd told her. Petra tried to stem the feeling of jealousy whenever Bernard visited him or the others who always seemed to congregate on these evenings. She didn't understand why Bernard preferred their company to hers. She'd always made herself available to discuss his work. She'd read copious amounts of books so she could engage with him more proficiently. Yet he'd stopped talking to her about his work at all.

The gap in the curtain allowed her a good view of the house without being seen herself. She was sat in the dark, in her bedroom, with Mr Gilman an accomplice on her lap. She was aware how it appeared, spying on her husband and his friends, peering through the curtains like a busy body. But she'd always felt there was something disconcerting about the neighbourhood. Something perplexing about Erich's house and the people that gathered there. She felt better keeping an eye out for Bernard waiting and watching for him to return with his briefcase in hand.

It was the briefcase that irked her the most. It was a customised case, designed to carry rocks and minerals securely. The fact he took it with him on these visits suggested that Bernard was showing Erich and the others something rare from one of the glass cabinets in his study, perhaps a gem Petra had seen before Bernard had become so secretive. Bernard especially prized his piece of stibrute with its gold filaments sharp and spiky like needles, or maybe it was the cloudy chalcedony that resembled the eggs of a huge spider. For a man so recently reticent about his work, to share his life's treasures with others felt like the ultimate betrayal.

She had tried to confront Bernard about it once but words get harder when you don't use them often enough, when you keep them buried for too long. They tumbled out disjointedly, a tirade of petty jealousy. It was unbecoming. Petra was ashamed. She resolved never to lose her reserve in front of Bernard again. He had never behaved like that in all their years together. He was like stone. She could be stone too.

The light went out in the house at the end of the street and Petra sank deeper into the chair as if she were suddenly visible. She watched Bernard leave by the front door, alone. He walked cautiously along the street, his head down and his collar up. As he got closer Petra realised the briefcase was gone.

Petra found herself walking toward the house at the end of the street. She'd waited for Bernard to settle in his study before retracing his steps from the previous evening. She rarely walked this way; the route to town was in the opposite direction. There was never any need to head towards the house, a building that was strangely situated in relation to the other houses; though the land it was built upon was flat, the street snaking towards it, it felt as if Erich's house marked some kind of summit.

As she walked, she became aware of how she was alone in not visiting the house. From her vantage in the upstairs bedroom, she often watched her neighbours strolling up towards Erich's house, emerging hours later. She'd always found Charles Erich to be cold and serious and couldn't imagine why people would want to spend time with him in his gloomy house. But Petra couldn't talk; she had no friends on the street to speak of. While Bernard was welcomed with open arms, it was almost as if there was a concerted effort to exclude her. And Petra wondered not for the first time whether it was Bernard's doing. That he didn't want his dowdy wife tagging along, that he wanted to keep his new friends all to himself.

Petra slowed her pace as she approached the building. She wasn't exactly sure what she was going to do. She had no intention of knocking the door and demanding Bernard's briefcase but neither was she going to retreat having come this close. Perhaps if she circled the building she might find what she was looking for.

The pavement stopped shy of Erich's lawn. A gravel path continued round to the back, but stepping onto it would be tantamount to trespassing. Petra cast a glance over her shoulder; there was nobody around. Erich's car wasn't parked in his drive. It would only take a moment.

The gravel scraped underfoot, giving her away. She made her way past dense shrubbery, overgrown and untended, and moved towards a window. The curtains were drawn but there was a small gap at the base. She bent down and peered in. Something small in the distance glinted, something gold or bronze, lustrous like metal or stone. But it was more than just polished; it was almost oily in consistency—or slimy.

Petra heard a sudden movement inside, footsteps across floorboards. She hastened back the way she had come, the gravel broadcasting her progress across the path. She was too old for this, she told herself, rounding the bend. She was nearly back on the pavement-

"Can I help you?"

Petra turned slowly to a man standing on the front porch. A tall man anyway, Charles Erich appeared even taller due to his elevated position on the porch. His arms were crossed; his countenance was steely, flinty. She had never understood why the other residents were so drawn to him when all she wanted to do was recoil. But she couldn't deny that he possessed a certain magnetism.

"Oh, goodness. You made me jump, Mr Erich."

The man stared but made no effort to move.

"I'm Petra, Bernard's wife," she continued, as if this explained matters. They'd met before, of course, but he looked at her now as if she were a complete stranger.

He nodded noncommittally.

"I'm terribly sorry to disturb you, but I'm looking for my cat. Mr Gilman. I don't suppose you've seen him?" Petra was surprised how readily the lie sprang to her lips. Mr Gilman had always been a housecat, even before age and infirmity had limited his movements.

Erich met her gaze as if he could dig for the truth there.

"I'm afraid I can be of no use to you. Perhaps you should get Mr Gilman a leash."

Petra wasn't sure whether he meant it as a joke, it was delivered so seriously, but she smiled politely and even managed a laugh. Erich turned and closed the door.

Petra stood outside the study. She wondered briefly about telling Bernard about her strange encounter with Erich, but it would be clear she'd lied about Mr Gilman. She'd only been allowed a cat on the proviso that it stayed indoors. At the time she'd assumed Bernard was just being protective, but now she wondered if it was really because he didn't want it snooping around the neighbourhood as she had done. Perhaps it was both. Curiosity killed the cat, after all.

Even though she had nothing to say, she found herself standing outside Bernard's study. His love for rocks had rubbed off on her too like chalk dust. She could feel the allure and pull of the study like a strange kind of magnetism. She knew some rocks were magnetic, like rhodonite and some varieties of garnet. Others had electronic properties like quartz and she wondered if it was some of this energy that lured her, not just the proximity of Bernard (though that was more likely).

Sometimes, when she stood outside like this, it was so quiet that she was often convinced Bernard wasn't there at all. She wondered if he was holding his breath on the other side, seeing her shadow beneath the door. She often imagined what it would be like if Bernard died. To be left alone in this big house with his locked room of secrets. She supposed she would have to find a way in. What she would do with all the minerals he'd accumulated in there she didn't know. Would the task of cataloguing rocks fall to her? Or would she return them to the ground with Bernard?

When Bernard went to the house at the end of the street that night, he went empty-handed. Petra watched for the re-emergence of the briefcase but again he returned home without it. Petra knew she couldn't quiz Bernard about it but she was curious about what he'd left in the care of Erich. She wondered, if she were to somehow gain entry to the study, whether she could tell what was missing from the glass cabinets. There was a time when she had studied the entire contents of Bernard's rock collection, drawn magpie-like to the assortment of rocks and gems. She may still be able to spot a missing item.

It wasn't the first time Petra had thought about breaking into Bernard's study. The impulse was strongest when Bernard first began locking her out. She was indignant that he was keeping her out of his life, suddenly concealing things from her. But she wanted to avoid confrontation; it seemed preferable to discover these things on her own.

There were practicalities to consider. She'd thought about picking the lock, but she worried about compromising the keyhole and about Bernard catching her in the act. No, there could be no traces of her transgression. She thought about trying to force the window and climbing through but it was street-facing and she risked being spotted by the neighbours, perhaps mistaken for a burglar. Plus she doubted she had enough physical strength at her age to haul herself up. The only feasible way was to somehow get hold of the key.

Bernard kept the key on him, except at night when he removed it from where it hung about his neck and placed it in his bedside drawer. He'd had a rose cut diamond set into the key face. The diamond had once belonged to a ring Bernard had found in an antiques shop, but he'd discarded the setting and band as if they were worthless. It was only the stone he was interested in. Petra wondered if he thought as little of his own wedding band.

She'd often considered how difficult it would be to

reach over and slide her hand into the drawer. She didn't know why she'd never attempted it before. Perhaps out of respect for his privacy or maybe a part of her didn't want to confront what was in the room.

Bernard had gone straight to bed when he returned home which was unusual. Normally he read until late in the study. Sometimes he read all night after visiting Erich, inspired, most probably, by something they'd discussed. But tonight he'd fallen into bed exhausted. Petra watched him sleep from the bedroom doorway, intrigued at how still he lay. In fact, he was unnaturally still, as if-

Petra edged closer, noting the rise and fall of Bernard's chest with relief, though he still had a certain eerie stillness about him. It wasn't a relaxed slumber at all; it was as if he were afraid to move.

Petra walked toward his side of the bed. If she was going to do it, this might be the only chance she had. She could take the key and go down to the study and finally face whatever demons Bernard had been hiding away in there. He need never know. She grasped the handle and pulled.

It was empty.

Petra looked to Bernard, expecting him to react to the sound of the drawer opening but he was as still as before. There was only one other place the key could be. She pulled the covers back slowly, trying not to disturb him. His hands were crossed against his chest and where they met they closed tightly about something.

The key.

Petra got into bed beside him and placed her hand over his.

PRECIOUS THINGS

Petra stood outside the door. She ran her hands along its surface, touching the brass handle and the keyhole. She ran her finger around the rim then pushed it into the empty space.

Something nipped her finger.

"Ouch."

Withdrawing it she saw a scratch along her fingertip. What could have been so sharp? She reached out her hand again and watched as something fibrous and long snaked out to meet her. It was almost translucent, like a thin needle of calcite or a ribbon helictite. But it coiled and curled as if it were organic.

Petra took a step back. Suddenly the keyhole was crowded with multiple stems, spiralling out vine-like towards her. And it wasn't just the keyhole. The door was iced over with a thick glaze of hoarfrost though the hall was uncomfortably hot, and Petra saw they were budding crystals, like the drusy that forms on the surface of a geode. The doorframe had begun to sprout nodes of basalt, rock crystal and cysts of quartz. Speleothems shot out towards her like blades, in seconds becoming formations that would have taken millennia. Finger-width stalactites hung like pendants from the doorframe and stalagmites rose from the floor, as soda straws wove themselves in and around the glistening stakes. There were smaller protrusions of gemstones that looked like aquamarine and spinel, ruby and garnet, obsidian and aragonite, decorating the doorframe as if it were a jewel-encrusted gateway.

Beneath the door, Petra watched stony shoots creep out, crystallising on route into other impossible structures, bursting into isometric and tetragonal formations like geometric flowers. Beyond that something wet and glutinous seeped out from beneath the door, like a puddle of molten gold. The same consistency of the thing she'd seen at the house at the end of the street, wet and slimy, bleeding its way towards her.

The door bowed under the pressure with an enormous sigh. The wood was hewed in half by a mighty conchoidal fracture, like the opening of a shell. What the earth relinquishes is often so beautiful, but not always. Petra stared as the door was ripped from its hinges, at the swelling darkness within.

Petra woke with a start. Bernard wasn't at her side, just a hollow indention of him in the bedding. Mr Gilman wasn't at her feet either, which was unusual as he normally compensated for Bernard's absence.

Petra got up and stretched, wishing she could shake off the feeling of the strange dream as easily. It was vague now, but she recalled crystals and gems, a treasure trove of precious things, though they left an unwanted residue in her mind.

She yawned, put on her slippers, and made her way downstairs. She was surprised Bernard was up so early and surprised, too, to hear Mr Gilman mewing as she made her way down the hall. And for a moment, she thought she heard the sound of splintering or scratching.

"Mr Gilman?" she cooed, "What are you up to?"

She saw Mr Gilman as she rounded the bend, clawing at the study door in frenzy.

Petra hurried towards him and Mr Gilman backed away as if thankful she was there to take over. Petra knew without trying the handle that Bernard was inside, and she knew with certainty he was in danger. She pounded the door with her hands, "Bernard! Bernard!"

She tried the handle again, wishing she had taken the key from Bernard when she'd had the chance. It was unyielding. She had no idea how she was going to get into the room, only that she had to. Bernard could be lying on the floor right now, the victim of a stroke or heart attack.

She looked around to see if there was anything she could use to pry the door open. She pounded the door again, getting a sense of the weight of it, wondering if she could run at it like firemen do in movies. She knew she didn't possess the strength, though. Once, maybe, but not now, not at her age. She kicked at the door, used her knees, knowing that she'd be bruised badly afterwards. She looked around for something better, cursing that she'd never given the idea of literally breaking in serious consideration, though she'd conceived of every other possible way into the room.

She needed something heavy, she realised, racing to a sideboard. Her eyes glanced over vases and picture frames before settling on a lamp. It was suitably weighty. Its base was a figurine—a mermaid—a garish bronzed and green thing. She'd chosen it to annoy Bernard, to elicit some kind of response, but he'd hardly noticed.

She ran back to the door, the cord dragging behind. She didn't even take the lampshade off. Holding the figurine below its shell-covered breasts, she drove it into the wood.

She was relieved when the wood creaked against the pressure. She redoubled her efforts, pounding the lamp base hard against the door. It was too heavy for her. She felt her fingers slip, her arms aching in way she hadn't felt for a long time. Mr Gilman meowed encouragement at her feet. She lifted the base again and hammered it like a battling ram. It was a battle, she reminded herself, Bernard was on the other side, alone. She needed to get in.

The mermaid split in two. Its tail fell to the floor, severed off as if relinquishing its aquatic existence. The lamp felt lighter in her hands, but insubstantial. She threw it aside and picked up the fishtail. She concentrated on the keyhole area, hoping to force the wood around it. It was a cheap door, typical of newer houses, and she thought what a mercy that was now. The plywood began to give, splintering in ways not unlike in her dream.

She used her shoulder for the rest. The door gave reluctantly and she stood on the threshold sweating and breathless.

It was dark. The blinds were down and the curtains were pulled shut. As her eyes became accustomed, she took in the room. It was not at all as she imagined.

In their previous homes, bookcases had lined the walls and glass cabinets were arranged in neat rows. Everything was catalogued and ordered. This room was chaos. The glass cabinets were pushed against the walls haphazardly, the stones inside scattered as if they were worthless. Books were strewn over the floor, the bookcases themselves upturned with other pieces of furniture. Petra couldn't even see Bernard's desk. And she couldn't see Bernard.

"Bernard!"

Petra made her way in the room, stepping over fallen items, gemstones dotted around like pebbles. Mr Gilman hesitated behind; he'd been so eager to get the door open but now wouldn't cross the threshold.

It looked as if the place had been ransacked but that was impossible. The window was secure and Petra could attest to the resilience of the door. Nobody could have gotten in here. This mess had to be of Bernard's making.

"Bernard," she called again, wading deeper into the disorder. "Bernard."

She heard a sound then. It was faint, the sound of stone, like footsteps on gravel. She headed towards it, stepping over books and furniture. A lopsided bookshelf blocked her way. It was propped up on its side as if it had been pulled down to form a barrier, or to make cover. Petra squeezed around it, surprised to see other pieces of furniture converged in a similar way, arranged like a strange tepee. Petra pulled a chair aside, books releasing clouds of dust as they fell to the ground. When the dust cleared Petra could see Bernard's desk in the centre.

His desk had been a matter of pride to him. It had belonged to a man of science before him and owning it had meant becoming part of its great legacy. Petra reached out to touch it when she felt a hand grasp at her ankle.

She screamed.

The hand withdrew under the desk. She stepped away first, then bent down on her already-bruised knees and peered into the darkness.

Bernard gazed back at her, though his eyes had a vague, far-away look she'd never seen before. And then Petra saw what he was doing. He was stirring a bowlful of pebbles and dirt with his finger. He twisted the bowl as if he were panning for gold, then crumbled the mix between his fingers looking for something elusive hidden between the grains. Then, clearly dissatisfied with just examining it by eye, he spooned it up into his mouth and began to chew, grounding the grit between his jaws. Petra made to object but Bernard's expression stopped her. It was the same look he had when he worked, when his mind was occupied with a problem. Petra could hear him crunching on stone, filtering the coagulated mass on his tongue, still hoping to find what he sought there. Then he looked at her and swallowed.

After a lot of coaxing, Petra managed to persuade Bernard up to bed. She tucked him beneath the covers and was relieved when he fell straight asleep. She knew this might not be the best recourse, but it had taken all her energy to get into the room and then to get Bernard up the stairs. She was exhausted. When she dialled for the doctor it struck her she had never called for help before. She could have easily called a neighbour or the emergency services, enlisted someone younger and stronger to get her into that room, yet it had never occurred to her.

She didn't want anyone to go into the room, she realised. It wasn't that she was ashamed of its current state—though she'd pulled the door closed on the mess as soon as Bernard was settled—it was because it was Bernard's private space. She'd been denied entry for so long, she wasn't about to open it up for *anyone* to see. She had no idea what secrets it housed yet, but she, above all others, had earned the right to know what they were.

Bernard woke complaining of the light.

"Does it hurt your eyes?" Petra asked as she turned it off, wondering what the doctor would make of it all. While she dressed in the dark she thought more fully about what she would tell the doctor, already erasing parts of the morning from the narrative she would tell. The doctor didn't need to know about the state of the study, or the fact she'd found Bernard chewing rocks, both of which couldn't signify anything other than a severe mental decline. It was enough to say she'd found him confused, unfocused.

It was an actual condition, Petra remembered, the rock-eating Bernard had been increasingly interested in it, back when he used to discuss his work with her over dinner. Pica disorder was an addiction for non-nutritive substances, in the same way pregnant women were known to eat clay when there wasn't enough iron in their diet. But pica denoted rocks and pebbles. Why would any sane person want to do that?

It made her think of mythological creatures—didn't dragons eat rocks? Did the stones somehow fuel or stoke the furnace in their stomachs? Trolls, she was sure, ate rocks but they also turned to stone, too. Did eating them hasten their metamorphosis?

Petra's head hurt. There had been lucidity to Bernard's behaviour. It was as if he were sifting the minerals, tasting them before he swallowed. Bernard was always so logical. Though she didn't understand it, there had to be method to his madness.

Bernard was taken in overnight as a precaution. They wanted to carry out a few more tests to be on the safe side, though the ones conducted already hadn't revealed anything out of the ordinary.

Petra had never been alone in the house before. Back from the hospital she didn't even remove her coat and shoes before making her way straight to the study, scared she might lose her nerve. She closed the door behind her, partly out of respect for Bernard's wishes, partly because it felt clandestine trespassing into his inner world.

Seeing it the second time was still a shock. Though she looked at scattered objects and books, she knew that really it was Bernard's state of mind that was on display. Perhaps that was his big secret—he'd lost his marbles. Petra nearly laughed at the irony; he'd lost more than marble! Quartz and ruby, garnet, sapphire and beryl were all scattered on the floor as if worthless. She stooped to pick them up, a precious trail of breadcrumbs leading deeper into the room.

She stopped at the desk again. This saddened her the most. Though her body ached, she bent down again and looked at the spot where she'd discovered Bernard. Having the study wasn't enough; he'd constructed a cave out of furniture, a smaller more private world than she could have imagined. Did he hate his life with Petra so much?

Petra hadn't noticed the rug underneath the desk, nor the darker wood it partly revealed, a contrast to the lighter floorboards that ran the length of the room. Petra pulled the rug aside, careful not to send Bernard's construction toppling. There was a handle. It was a trap door.

Petra had to move all of the furniture to open it. It was laborious. Bernard had made sure to keep it weighted down—like a strange guardian. Bernard wasn't here now though and Petra had come this far. She couldn't shy away from knowing the truth. She gripped the handle and, using what strength she had left, heaved it open.

Darkness. And then, as her eyes became accustomed, a stairwell. It was crudely made but perfectly serviceable. It didn't occur to her not to follow it. Bernard's secret world was open now. The damage was already done.

She took the stairs cautiously. They led on to a narrow corridor. She followed it, the light from the study diminishing with every step. When she was in complete darkness she stood for a moment waiting for her eyes to adjust. Slowly her surroundings came into focus.

It was a corridor with a little anteroom. She could see overalls hanging up from a nail in the wall. Tools were arranged neatly, pickaxes and hammers, maps and blueprints tacked to the walls. It looked like some strange mining station.

Petra couldn't believe what she was seeing. How

had she not known this space was below their house? Had Bernard been down here all this time when she was imagining him hunched over his books in the study. Why had he never shared it with her?

Petra examined the tools and reached for a torch but it was busted. She reached for another and saw it was the same. The Perspex lenses were either cracked or their batteries had been removed. Petra picked up some batteries off the floor and tried them anyway, surprised when one of the broken torches spluttered to life. It was unlike Bernard not to take care of his things.

The light from the cracked glass was fragmented, providing a distorted view of the corridor ahead. She almost missed a second staircase, having to grab the walls to stop from falling. The torch fell from her hands, illuminating further depths as it bounced against stone steps on its way down. Stone steps—this part had to be older than the first section she'd been in.

She reached the bottom and bent to retrieve the torch. She was too old for this. Bernard was too old for this. He'd been descending deeper and deeper into the earth all these years, while Petra was doing his laundry or preparing dinner. Picking up the torch, its beam caught a dark shape ahead, low to the ground.

Petra recoiled and the shape shrank from the light. She held the torch firmer, outstretched her arm and brandished the beam across the width of the tunnel as if it were a weapon.

A rat? No, it was too big for a rat and Petra knew it. Besides, it had slithered out of the way, as a snake would. Petra held the torch firm. She tried to control her breathing.

PRECIOUS THINGS

"Hello?" She wasn't sure this was such a good idea. She edged forward. The tunnel seemed to be empty.

It definitely was an established tunnel, hewn into the stone. Very old, by the looks of it, vastly different to the wooden corridor just below their house. That had to have been built more recently, to feed into this one. Petra found herself recalling what she knew of the local area. Perhaps it was part of an old mining duct, or an escape route from an abbey or castle during the Reformation. But her mind drew a blank.

She continued along its path and thought perhaps it was snaking downwards. She remembered all those times she'd waited and listened on the other side of the study door, oblivious that Bernard was trekking further and further from their home.

She stopped. She'd heard something. It wasn't just the sound of her footsteps on the stone steps. She listened hard, afraid to move in case it masked it. There it was. A rattling of sorts but with a deeper, grainier texture. Stony. Petra sighed. She was underground after all; maybe it was normal for a bit of subsidence. She was reminded of the sound of Bernard crunching on his concoction of pebbles and dirt, the way his finger had stirred the mixture. The sound of a multitude of stones rubbing against one another. Except this was more violent, more urgent. And getting louder. It suddenly sounded like a landslide, the earth yawning open and crying out.

Petra ran back the way she had come. She was convinced now the tunnel had led her downwards because she could feel the upward gradient as she tried to make her way back, her legs aching. The sound was behind, gaining on her. Her logical mind told her it couldn't be a landslide; that gravity wouldn't allow the earth to surge upwards. Yet she could feel whatever it was following her. Could feel its immediacy at her heels.

She turned as she ran, shining the torch back the way she had come. Its beam revealing dark shadows creeping around the circumference of the tunnel. Petra watched as the forms slithered out, dark glutinous shapes that followed behind. Petra ran faster. She could see the stone staircase up ahead.

She climbed as fast as she could, then along the corridor under their house, past Bernard's equipment, up the second staircase.

The trapdoor was shut.

She'd closed it behind her on her way down. She fiddled with the latch, flustered. Her hands didn't have the grip they used to. She cursed her old age. She shone the torch in front of her, watching the dark thing snake up the corridor. I'm too old to run, she told herself, and a feeling of relief swept over her. Acceptance. It didn't matter what happened to her, who would care if she were gone? Certainly not Bernard, with his mind obsessed, irredeemably it seemed, with rocks.

She thought of Mr Gilman crying and scratching on the trapdoor as he'd done when Bernard was in danger. Who'd feed Mr Gilman? He was a housecat; if anything happened to her, he'd be entombed within the house forever.

Petra gripped the handle and pushed with all her might. The hatch fell open with a thud and the musty smell of Bernard's study welcomed her. She ran up the remaining steps, clutching the trapdoor, and shone the torch back into the ground. Before she closed the hatch, she saw the space beneath filled with a writhing black mass, like a river of shadows.

Bernard was brought home the next day, tucked in bed and propped up with pillows. "The light," he said again. Petra turned the bedside lamp off and he fell straight to sleep. Exhausted no doubt from his ordeal over the last few days. Petra knew how he felt. She sat at his bedside and held his hand.

"Oh, Bernard."

She brushed the hair from his face: the colour of marble or chalk. Even in sleep, his face was stern, unmoving. The lines on his face were like crevices in rock, hardened into permanence. She understood why his condition couldn't be explained by any test. He was being ground down under an enormous weight. Of the thing he had discovered—awoken. It was written on his face.

Petra got into the bed beside him and tried not to think about the thing in the tunnel, though it was impossible. She hoped it was a hallucination, the result of a panic attack in such a confined space, the stress of Bernard being poorly. But she knew she had experienced something malevolent, some dark force beneath their home. And Bernard had, too. She wanted to wake him and tell him he didn't need to worry, that she could help carry this burden. She'd been into his private world and come out the other side.

But Bernard slept soundly. He didn't look like the same man she'd seen under the desk, stirring the bowl madly as if it were a cauldron. His countenance was stonier now, determined.

Petra traced her finger over his forehead. There was something enduring about him, something stoic about his appearance. Petra couldn't imagine him decomposing when he died, breaking down organically like everyone else. Becoming food for worms. No, he would lie exactly where he was, and over time, his pores would begin to sprout carbonate formations, quartz grains would gather in the creases of his skin and crystals would grow from his laughter lines, decorating his smile and the corners of his eyes as if to compensate for his serious demeanour. He would develop a carapace of sandstone and shale, becoming part of the landscape, subject to the winds and rain and the unhurried passing of time. Her rock.

Petra woke to a knocking at the door. It surprised her; they rarely had visitors. She made her way downstairs with Mr Gilman at her heels, pausing at a mirror to ensure there were no tell-tale signs of sleep. Napping in the day was a sign of getting old.

She opened the door.

"Mr Erich," she said, trying to sound as cheerful as possible. "Good morning."

"Good afternoon," he corrected her, taking any opportunity to assert his control. "I see you found your cat."

Petra looked at Mr Gilman curled about her feet.

"Yes, yes, he turned up again, thank goodness." Erich wasn't the kind of man to pay social calls and Petra wasn't in the mood to feign politeness for long. "What can I do for you?"

"Is Bernard around? He missed our last meeting and my sources tell me they saw an ambulance parked here yesterday."

Sources? Petra knew she wasn't the only busy body in the neighbourhood, but sources? She wondered if the whole community were Erich's minions.

"I'm afraid Bernard's resting just now. He had a fall. Nothing serious, thankfully. I'll tell him you called"

"It's just that Bernard and I had been talking about some rather serious work. I wondered if I might have a quick look in the study. Retrieve some of my notes."

Petra felt her hold of the door tighten. "I don't think so. Bernard is very particular about his study. He has a very organised way of working." She realised as she began to close the door all that had changed. "But I'll be sure to pass on your message."

Erich put his hand out to stop the door. Mr Gilman fled back down the hall. "It will only take a moment."

He looked past her then, along the hallway to the study. She wondered if he could see the busted door from where he stood. He would know she'd been inside, and she wondered then how much he knew about Bernard's work and about how much he thought *she* knew.

Erich looked at her intently, his gaze boring into her, trying to excavate the truth. She could feel the pull of the study, its magnetic energy. Erich could probably feel it, too, and for a moment she thought he was going to rush at her, push her aside.

He could try. She stepped forward, barring his way.

"This isn't a good time," she said firmly. "Bernard will be up and about in a few days." She hoped that was true. "I'll get him to contact you."

Before Erich could say any more, she shut the door.

Petra stood outside the study door, waiting for her breathing to slow, the rage to pass. She'd always had a bad feeling about Erich. How could Bernard be friends with a man like that? Had Erich intimidated Bernard? Threatened him, perhaps? She thought of the way Erich had looked past her. She was insignificant, an obstacle to be surmounted, a mere old lady, and she knew with a certain feeling of dread he would be back. That he would find a way into Bernard's study.

She could call the police but they'd pass her story off as dementia. Besides, Erich had friends everywhere. No, if she was going to help Bernard she needed to understand what it was Erich wanted from that room.

She opened the door slowly. She hadn't been back in there since her flight from the tunnels. She'd have rather never stepped inside again. In fact she'd rather leave this place and the strange neighbourhood for good. But the room lured her with its strange energy and with its secrets temptingly within reach. Since breaking the door down her curiosity had swelled and grown like the thing in the tunnels. She couldn't leave without knowing.

PRECIOUS THINGS

She didn't open the curtains or the blinds; she didn't want Erich or his friends peeking in. She switched on the overhead light and moved to the centre of the room where a heap of furniture converged over the trapdoor. A similar construction to the one Bernard had built. Hers was a lot more impromptu but it had sufficed. She walked around the room slowly now, hoping she could find what it was she sought without disturbing the barricade in the centre.

She started in the glass cabinets and bookcases, the gemstones piled up like sparkling cairns. The bookcases yielded even less, dusty tomes written in dense scientific language. She rifled through books on mineralogy and gemology, periodicals on mineralogical discoveries and journals on lapidary equipment. It was Bernard's language; she couldn't discern any meaning there.

She moved onto the sideboards and filing cabinets, rummaging in drawers and opening cupboards. There had to be something that pointed her in the right direction but the contents were just as disordered. She sat on the floor and looked around in dismay. There was no system here, no order, no answers. Or if there ever was, there wasn't anymore.

Petra picked up a lamp that was lying on the floor beside her. The least she could do was clean it up a bit. She placed the lamp back in its rightful place and turned it on.

A series of indiscernible line drawings appeared before her, etched into the upturned surfaces of the cabinet's glass. Petra could make out the scribbled markings, gossamer-thin scratched into the glass. She ran her finger over one indentation, the glass splinters catching on her skin. It would've been made by something sharp. The diamond on Bernard's key. Of course! He'd loved the story that Elizabeth the First used to etch love messages to her suitors on the windows of her palaces with her diamond 'scribbling ring'—Bernard had found a similar use for his.

Petra lifted the lamp and held it closer to Bernard's secret. With the light at a certain angle, Petra saw the entire length of glass was covered in one huge image.

She recoiled. Nearly dropped the lamp.

It looked like a kraken. Some ocean creature stretching out its serpentine limbs like a mythological beast. And there were annotations pointing towards sections of the illustration.

It wasn't just a picture she realised; it was a map. What she'd taken for limbs were actually tunnels, eight of them, joining at a large central point.

Petra noticed some of the tunnels were shaded, covered in messy crosshatchings that still left filaments of glass on the surface. Petra considered the tunnel she'd discovered beneath their home. Perhaps Bernard had shaded the parts he'd traversed. It made sense. He'd begun at various tunnel ends but never the centre. Did that mean there were other access points across the neighbourhood? One tributary was more shaded than the others, which she assumed to be the one directly below their home, but it stopped just shy of the core.

Petra stared into the glass. According to the map, the whole neighbourhood was built on a network of ancient tunnels. How many people knew about it? Is that why such an unassuming suburbia had developed on top? Did Bernard know? Did Erich?

Petra placed the lamp down. Of course they knew. It was why they were here. Why they arranged their little meetings. Bernard had been tempted by the ultimate treasure, and he had a map. How could he resist?

Petra thought about the layout of the street, considered how the new buildings would appear from the air. Gauging the distance from their house to Erich's, she was pretty certain his house would stand directly above the heart of the tunnel system.

If Erich already knew about the tunnels, he didn't need a map, which meant he wanted something else from the room. But the fact Bernard had gone to such lengths to etch it into glass implied it wasn't meant to be seen. The indentations were only visible in the light and it looked as if Bernard had kept the room habitually dark. It was supposed to remain a secret.

Petra knelt closer to the glass, holding the lamp as near as possible, in case there was something else she had missed. In between the annotations she saw a list of gemstones: spinel, tourmaline, amethyst, yellow turquoise, beryl, unakite, rhodonite, iolite, emerald, diamond. It was an unusual list. There had to be a reason why they were written down. Perhaps they had similar properties, the same atomic structure or something, but Petra drew a blank. Maybe the list had something to do with the Mohs scale, indicating a stone's hardness. Diamond scored the highest on the scale and emerald wasn't much further down but Petra wasn't sure about the rest of the order, and didn't know what it would signify anyway.

She wrote the list on her hand with one of the discarded fountain pens scattered on the floor and continued with her search, discovering the list repeated twice more on one glass cabinet, and three more times on another.

Bernard disliked repetition. Why exhaust yourself with the same words, he'd argue, when in the early days Petra had complained that he didn't say he loved her often enough. If the sentiment remained the same, why verbalise it again? Yet, here was the same list repeated, over and over. Maybe Bernard had lost his marbles after all.

There didn't seem to be any logic to the placement of the lists either. They were scattered on various glass surfaces and even etched into a couple of wooden ones. Petra didn't know how she'd missed them; they stared out at her now as if the veil on an invisible world had suddenly been lifted.

She ran her hands over the front of Bernard's desk. The list ran along the length of the table edge, like a long sentence stopping at 'emerald' because Bernard had run out of room. Petra knelt underneath the desk, in the same position she'd found him only a day ago. Then she looked up at the underside of the desk and half-felt, half-read the word 'diamond.'

As she touched the word again, she realised the wood it was etched on was hollow. You'd never know from the front of the desk, the surface appeared so flat, yet she could feel a panel, the possibility of a concave space behind it. Petra strained her eyes, pressing her fingers firmly against the wood.

She heard a clear tap as she added pressure and she felt the wood panel open. She pulled it across. It didn't extend far but the gap was sufficient for her to slide her hand up and into the base of the desk. Her hand went deeper into the compartment and brushed against fabric. She pulled out something bundled in thick cloth.

She opened it.

Her first instinct was to drop it. But she also knew it was precious. She could feel its worth in the weight in her palm. Not that it was anything special to look at, a dull black stone the shape of a large teardrop. It looked like natural glass in parts and Petra could well imagine it being caused by the impact of a meteorite. It was sharp at the edges and it had a craggy texture like stone, like tektite more specifically. It was the same colour of the thing she'd seen in the tunnels and for a moment she almost convinced herself she held a part of the that writhing mass in her hands, a piece somehow made solid.

Petra was about to place it down when she felt it warming up in her hands. She thought briefly of jet, the stone made popular for mourning centuries before, its thermal properties well suited for warming the cold hearts of the recently bereaved. But it was heavier than jet and jet wasn't known to flash amber. Petra watched in amazement as the stone began to change colour, no longer black at all but blazing gold, its centre swirling like molten gold, the colour of the thing she had seen at Erich's house. It glowed in her hands, a strange otherworldly beacon.

As the light shone Petra found her mind conjuring strange images. She saw a woman in old-fashioned clothing lying in the centre of a stone circle, her hands bound and a glowing stone at her feet. A wild darkness swirled above her head before it obscured her entirely. When it eventually moved away, like a fog dissipating, all that was left of the woman was her calcified remains. Then Petra saw the stone circle was replaced by a group of men. One of them moved into the centre and scattered the woman's ashes about with his foot, stamping her remains into the ground. There was something familiar about his bearing, about his flinty countenance.

Petra put the stone down and almost at once its inner light began to diminish. Within a few seconds it was the colour it had been before. Petra had never experienced anything like it. The golden light had been so beautiful, so alluring and she wanted to touch it again, but she couldn't endure again the images it had put in her mind.

She knew without any doubt that this stone was what Erich sought. She noticed there were other smaller black chunks wrapped up in the fabric, perhaps pieces that had crumbled free. Petra regarded these portions knowing if she touched them they'd resembled nuggets of gold. Like Midas's touch. Perhaps this was what Bernard had been showing them at Erich's house, smaller pieces of the whole.

"Oh Bernard." He should have known better than to have shown off his precious things.

Petra left Mr Gilman an abundance of cat food. She hoped he wouldn't gorge himself. There was enough for a couple of days, when a health visitor was expected to check on Bernard. Petra didn't want to think of the worst but it was better to be prepared. After she'd petted Mr Gilman, she climbed the stairs to Bernard.

PRECIOUS THINGS

He wasn't sleeping now but neither did he appear fully awake. It was almost as if he were in a daze or stupor. He didn't seem to notice her as she sat alongside him.

"Darkness," he said.

"Yes dear, it's dark in here; I've turned the lights off." She took his hand and without meaning to started to cry.

She allowed the tears to fall unrestrained and when she could cry no more she imagined her tears crystallising there on her checks, hardening into stone. She removed the chain with the key from Bernard's neck. He lay inert, unresponsive to her touch. She slipped it over her head. She'd always wanted a diamond. Diamond was the superlative stone, a symbol of perfection. Petra thought of the discovery in Bernard's desk. X marks the spot. The word 'diamond' had pointed towards something equally, if not more, precious.

The diamond was small, now scuffed and blunted, testament to the number of clandestine scrawls in Bernard's study. Petra compared it to the gems of her engagement ring, stones Bernard had selected himself, though less costly. Just as precious in her eyes as any diamond. What was diamond but carbon anyway? Perhaps that was why they were forever. Petra suddenly thought of the carbon in a human body, and the woman from her vision, her body reduced to a pile of dust.

She moved to the window and looked out at the street. A group of people had converged outside one of the houses; the house belonging to the young couple who'd lost their boy in the car accident. In the aftermath, Petra had wanted to offer her condolences but the woman's stony countenance had always kept her at bay. The young man seemed nice enough, though. In fact, she'd felt a strange affinity towards him, as if they both were somehow trapped in a world they didn't understand. She'd wished she had spoken to him now. She felt an ominous certainty that it was too late.

The crowd on his front lawn began to disperse. She watched them move slowly up the street. She knew where they would be heading.

Petra removed her engagement ring and left it on Bernard's bedside table, something precious to remember her by. She held his diamond in her palm. It was an exchange of rings, not unlike the one that had taken place all those years ago.

Dearest.

Petra looked at her hand without its ring. Not as empty as she thought it would look with the list of gemstones she'd scribbled there, copied from Bernard's study.

It was so blatantly obvious now that Petra couldn't believe she'd missed it. It was another acronym. Bernard always had preferred the language of stone.

Spinel. Tourmaline. Amethyst. Yellow turquoise. Beryl. Unakite. Rhodonite. Iolite. Emerald. Diamond.

STAY BURIED.

Petra entered the tunnels for a second time in complete darkness. She carried the strange stone, wrapped in thick cloth, in her satchel. She couldn't afford to touch it, to ignite the strange light that came from human contact. She realised now the darkness was drawn to it. That was why Bernard had destroyed the torches, blacked out his study, insisted on darkness in their home. And why the darkness had followed her up the tunnel that day. It craved the light and the stone's unnatural light in particular. Bernard had taken away the one thing that pacified it. And now it was up to her to put it back.

She hoped it would be obvious where Bernard had taken it from, that he'd left some clues as to where it had been found. She hoped by returning it she could mollify whatever forces lurked beneath the neighbourhood.

The tunnel wound deeper into the ground. Petra had come further than before. Her footsteps reverberated, echoing off stone to fill the tunnel. It sounded as if the whole underground system was alive.

She walked faster.

The tunnel began to narrow. Barely noticeable at first, Petra seemed to suddenly find herself stooping. She could feel the walls closing in on each side, the tunnel constricting around her. She thought for the first time about the tons of earth above her head, about the possibility of them caving in and trapping her down here forever. She'd read somewhere the Victorians were obsessed with the idea of being buried alive. Little bell mechanisms were fitted to coffins so if you woke up in the ground you could ring for assistance. Petra could only scream if she needed help and she doubted if anyone did happen to hear that they'd come. She was as alien to this community as the thing in her satchel was to her. Erich and his friends would probably rather see her buried. It was Bernard who'd been invited into their community, not her.

She was relieved when she stepped out into a large space, though it was short-lived when she realised it was the epicentre, a cavernous room, a huge underground grotto. Petra looked around the periphery. She could see entrances to other tunnels, narrow doorways surrounding her as she walked into the middle of the chamber, aware now of strange formations that converged there. They resembled stalagmites except much wider and larger than was typical, as tall as her. They rose from the ground in bulbous rod-like mounds. Petra touched the one closest, its surface wet but not cold as she expected. Surprisingly warm, in fact.

Petra stepped back a few feet and noted their arrangement. They formed a near perfect stone circle, a strange megalithic structure. Petra knew how mathematical the earth could be, patterns within the biology of plants that were intricately mapped, crystals that were geometrically and symmetrically perfect, but she'd never seen structures like this organised in such a way. It had to be engineered. For a moment she wondered if they were stone at all.

Stone circles were sacred, she knew as much. If this was the epicentre, there was only one place something precious belonged.

She touched another one as she moved to the middle. This time she could feel its warmth like a pulse, could feel its glow. She stared at it; it had a kind of humanoid appearance. It almost looked like a group of men standing in a circle. Petra shivered remembering her vision.

PRECIOUS THINGS

She made her way to the middle of the circle and knelt down, undoing her satchel. She removed the item and unwrapped it, setting it in the middle like an offering.

Petra found herself thinking about precious things. How can they be measured or calculated when love of a thing is so subjective? Precious stones, she knew, were rated according to a number of factors. Beauty, durability and rarity. The most precious were the ones at the top of that list, diamond, ruby, sapphire. Petra had always thought of herself as amethyst, something pleasing but mid list, something that could be made to sparkle if looked after. Beauty, she knew, depended on the skill of the cutter and polisher, and on the way the light brought out the colours. But over the years, throughout their marriage, she'd lost her lustre. She felt as dull as flint. For Bernard there was always something else to discover, something else of potentially greater worth.

Petra stood. She thought of Bernard in their bed, knowing with certainty he'd never be the same again. Deathly still, he'd become stone like the mounds that surrounded her. But why hadn't she been similarly affected by her time in the tunnels? Surely she'd been exposed to the same thing he had? Perhaps she was more resilient than him after all? And then she remembered Bernard's bowlful of pebbles and rocks, she remembered him eating the strange concoction as if he were working it all out.

Petra looked at the ground, where all of Bernard's passion, his *obsession*, came from. The surface of the inner circle differed from the stone of the tunnels. The ground here was comprised of tiny particles, pebbles and dirt, finely ground. Petra knelt, crumbling the mixture between her fingertips and she knew then with an eerie certainty that this was the same substance Bernard had eaten. And remembering her vision, she knew, too, that there were more than just rocks at the heart of it.

A rush of movement. Vibrations shot up from the ground startling her. From under her feet strange pulses of energy. The rocks trembled, small pebbles and rocks impacting with increasing volume. It was as if she were standing on a loudspeaker, the rocks juddering with fury, leaping higher and higher.

Spots of darkness coiled out of the tunnel entrances as if summoned by the strange sound, by the earth itself. Darkness slithered towards the circle. She turned on the spot, knocking the idol at her feet and it began to glow gold.

She thought briefly of her life on the other side of the door. It had been a good life. Though she'd never had all of Bernard, she'd had a part of him and for a long while that had been enough. But he'd given himself away, long before he'd unearthed the thing in the tunnels. He'd only ever been devoted to rocks, to what resided in the ground.

Around her the stone formations began glowing, too. She could see vaguely familiar shapes inside, swimming molten gold inside stony cocoons. Some minerals were known to temporarily change colour, but this was more than just tenebrescence, they were beacons for the darkness and she realised their light illuminated her in the centre.

Beauty, durability, rarity. Beauty needs light, and her beauty was lit up by the slow treacle glow of the stones. As for durability, what is marriage but a test of resilience? Toughened by those years, and by the events of the last few days as the bruises on her knees and arms attested, she was stronger than she had ever given herself credit. Stronger than Bernard, who had given in to Erich and his followers, consuming the rocks to transform into what they wanted him to be, another devotee to the darkness, part of their inner circle. As for rarity, well she suddenly saw what Bernard had seen that day he'd found her on the beach.

She was one of a kind.

The stone circle blazed. Petra wondered if Bernard had tried to keep her out all these years, on the other side of the door, because he wanted to protect her from what he'd found in the earth, from what he saw in himself. Maybe he'd kept her in the dark because she was the most precious thing after all.

She turned and faced the light.

MEAT, MOTION AND LIGHT

ROSANNE RABINOWITZ

CLAUDIA GAZES AT the image carved along one wall of the old chapel, a many-limbed sea creature spread against a stony suggestion of waves and seaweed. Part of the National Trust estate, this chapel has become something of a tourist attraction since she left Priory.

Years ago, she told another little girl that she had seen the *real* creature swimming around and she'll show it to her if she came to her house . . . A familiar tightness gathers around Claudia's chest, warning of an impending panic attack.

Her therapist suggested that many of her memories were symbolic. But symbols stand for real things, *of course* . . .

"Hello, Sucker-mucker," she whispers. Making up names for this thing should put her in a better frame of mind.

She tries to slow down her breathing. Is this nothing more than a quaint artefact? That's right, just like the Mermaid of Zennor and the whole crew of sheela-na-gigs, green men and gargoyles. She touches the surface. These days the restored carving is polished and preserved against the sticky fingers of schoolchildren.

There's a pebble-like effect to the underside of an extended tentacle, becoming more defined and sucker-like towards the tip. Claudia jabs her finger into the hollow of a stone sucker. It sends a chill up her backbone as it brings back last night's dream, one of those stupid dreams about being a child and your grown-up self at the same time . . .

She is walking down the street at Priory. The sun is shining, reflecting off the pale walls of the houses, so bright it hurts her eyes. It bleaches everything out, except for the brown of her skin. As usual, it's silent here, even when people come out of the houses.

They stare at her as if they've never seen anyone like her before.

Claudia looks around for her mother, but she's not there.

Of course, she's away on a trip. Out to sea.

Then the people of Priory start throwing rocks. When they hit, they open up and turn slick and sucker-like, part stone and part flesh. She tries to pull one off, but it won't budge. As she struggles, more stones hit her and attach themselves and merge with her skin . . .

She shakes her head to get those thoughts out, and flicks her finger against a carved sucker on the wall. The unknown artists who created it didn't get this detail quite right. They're not hollow like that, not at all.

Behind the creature the stone is smooth and dark

grey on one side, on the other it is rough with quartz and mica, glinting in the afternoon sun. A fractured oval shape joins the two sides while spreading open, a widening rip in the fabric of the sea.

"This background shows how our Nameless One stands between the worlds," Caitlin used to proclaim to the children of Priory, bangles jangling as she gestured to the wall. "This ancient carving proves that even those who profess Christianity have worshipped him and paid him homage."

Along with other children from Priory, Claudia was sent to a private school that allowed the enclave to pursue its own religious education, with Caitlin as their very own RE teacher.

Visiting the chapel had been an approved activity, yet it offered opportunities to get out of Priory, walk along the coastal path where the sea is rough and noisy rather than dark and concealing.

There were also opportunities to talk to outsiders at a tea shop near the church, and a pub just down the path. Teenagers from the community managed to sneak off for a quick half, though the elders of Priory instigated regular crackdowns with complaints about under-age drinking at the pub.

Claudia had taken advantage of the loophole offered by this allegedly sacred site. Gone to the pub with Roddy Jones for that quick half and an even quicker session in the woods. Or she'd knock back an alcopop with his sister Theresa, who had also introduced her to old punk music: *"Priory is burning with boredom now,"* they sang along with the Clash.

Priory could book the chapel for private services and talks, but an hour's hire wasn't enough for some. When the new Conservative government made plans to flog national parks and numerous national trust properties, the elders of their community were first in line to buy that chapel. Then storms of public protest ultimately cancelled the massive sell-off.

This confirmed Charles Erich's view that Priory had enough bankers and needed more lawyers. So Claudia might have been a bit gobby and dyed her hair blue or pink, but did well enough academically to get packed off to law school.

Or maybe her mother had something to do with it.

Now that she's up close to the carving, Claudia notices a scrawling on the wall. *Fuck off. Give it horsemeat. No, I like horses. Feed it Ian Duncan Smith and let it choke.* Damn, there's graffiti on the sacred site!

She's sure only youngsters from Priory could have written it, and no one would've dared do that in her day. The sight puts a cheerful crack in her grim resolve and makes her laugh.

A few teenagers stand at the edge of the woods near the path, watching her. "What's so funny?" one shouts, amid their own mocking laughter.

The boys and girls slouch, their body language speaking of flirtation and defiance.

There was none of *that* when I was young, Claudia

thinks. *None of that.* Among her few friends, there was only covert rebellion. It mainly involved having sex as soon as possible, as much as possible, with the slogan of a popular film in mind: if you haven't had it, you've had it. In the films, virgins were always getting sacrificed. It seemed a good excuse to indulge, even though they knew that their resident monster didn't give a shit about anyone's sex life.

Claudia goes over to the kids. "All right?"

"Who the fuck are you?"

But then a girl recognises her. "Oh, yes, I know who you are. You babysat for me a few times. You have the psycho-mum who talks to the thing."

"Yup, that's my mum."

Claudia babysat for a few kids when she was a teenager. They were all miserable brats. The one she's talking to . . . Roberta, that's her name. She once saw a book that Claudia was reading—Richard Dawkins—and threatened to report her for insubordination and heresy, though those weren't the words she used. Good to see that the little swot and snitch might be turning out OK, after all.

"So you went away and came back? You're crazy. I'd do anything to get out of here."

Claudia sighs. "You can get out, but you can't get away for good. Unless . . ."

For a while, she believed she could live a normal life. University, girlfriend, singing in a band . . . Then her mother wanted her back over the summer, for something "crucial and wonderful."

"You'll understand why we came to Priory."

No. *You* went to Priory and dragged me along, Claudia continues the everlasting mental row with her mother. Took me away from familiar streets and friends and freedom. Cut me off from family I've only just rediscov—

"I've seen your band on YouTube," the girl interrupts her unfinished sentence. "It's not bad . . . not bad."

"Thanks," says Claudia. 'Not bad' can be a great compliment.

"You shouldn't have come back," adds the girl.

"I had to."

No, that summons from Mum is a relentless reminder she won't ever live a real life outside the walls. Each night, there was the turning and churning of her thoughts. Constant, constant. And finally, the dreams . . . until she wakes up to sun streaming through the curtains, stabbing behind her gritty eyes. The whine of tiredness settles in as soon as she remembers where she is and who she is. Days feel used and wrung out before they begin, tasting of dried blood and dishwater.

"Why?" Roberta asks. "Do you think you'll change anything? Our friend has disappeared, and you know what that means. The same can happen to you . . . or me."

Tense conversation breaks out among the teenagers about their friend. About the friend's parents, joining with others to challenge Charles Erich.

Claudia is relieved to hear that 'psycho-mum' Lorraine is on the right side.

"Having a go at that disgusting old tosser."

"That fucking disgusting old shite," adds a boy.

Claudia stifles an impulse to go *shshh*. She and Theresa used to sing about Priory burning with boredom, but they wouldn't have talked out loud that way about Charles Erich . . . not even after several Moscow Mules.

Claudia continues to postpone her approach to Priory, stopping for a coffee in Exham. The handsome seaside town is busy on a warm day, during a most unusually summer-like British summer.

But despite the crowds, there are few other black people on the street. When she first moved to this area, it was worse. She and her mother were the *only* black people in the town as well as in the nearby enclave of Priory.

"What century do these people live in?" Lorraine used to ask in the beginning. "You'd think it was the 1890s, not the 1990s, going by those looks they give us!"

Now Claudia can count about three non-white faces here. Wait . . . She amends the count to four as a black policewoman crosses the street towards the café. The policewoman catches Claudia's eye in the window for a moment, then looks away.

Claudia pushes some stray hair from her face, which suddenly feels too warm.

She's toned down the Afropunk look for this visit, let the deep pink colour wash out and tied back her chaotic natural hair, but there's still a hint of rose in its brightly bleached mass. Despite her efforts she still attracts attention. After all, she's not simply a black woman, but a young black woman with pink-tinted hair who makes no effort to look like Beyoncé.

Better get used to it, girl. You'll be on your own at Priory—unless you count your mum.

Claudia pushes her frothy cappuccino aside, and puts her head in her hands as she remembers another dream. That damn carving on the chapel must have brought it back . . .

Her mother is showing Claudia the creature, showing her the window where they can watch it. But this time the creature watches them, too, and the window is filled with its eye.

It is huge, but surprisingly human. It reminds her of the eye of a very old man, even older than her grandfather. Folds of flesh surround it, and there's a filmy cast over the eyeball.

When she actually *saw* that eye her mother was holding her hand, reassuring her it wasn't the eye of a monster. It belonged to a fabulous creature larger and more complex than any that roamed the Earth's surface. Claudia wasn't scared then, in real life.

But in her dream, she is terrified.

The gelatinous film over the eye, almost a mist, is full of fleeting facets and images. Some are so strange her mind can't record what they are.

She tries to look away to avoid the sights trapped within the eye. If she sees them, she will die. But she has no control. Her head is being turned so she has to look. She has no choice but to see . . .

"Get outta my head. Get outta my fucking head," she whispers to herself.

No putting her visit off any longer. She gulps down the cappuccino, remembering her mother only drinks herbal tea. Then she pays and leaves.

Nigel, who looks after the gate, comes out of his discreet control room to say hello when she arrives. Claudia nods. Nigel has his good points. Back in her days as a pissed-off Priory teenager, he wasn't above bribery when you wanted a night out. No doubt those kids near the woods have greased his palm a few times.

When she first moved here, members of the community used to share the security and maintenance tasks because they didn't trust outsiders with them. Then they decided they were all too busy making money or communing with denizens of the deeps, so they hired Nigel after recruiting him at a David Icke seminar. His distrust of reptiles never extended to cephalopods, or things that look like cephalopods.

"Haven't seen you in a while," Nigel says. "Things have gone downhill here, but something's stirred up, too." He winks, assuming she's in on the same conspiracy.

"I know nothing about that, but I guess I'll find out. See you later." As the gate closes behind her, Claudia turns to face her home town.

Priory consists of streets fanning out from a main road, with Charles Erich's mansion and the community centre in the middle. In contrast to the sharp rises and dips of the coastal path, it's absolutely flat here.

She notices some newly built houses on each side of the main street, though one is empty and boarded up. Claudia left Priory in 2009, just after the crash, and it looks like the recession is showing its face even here.

No one plays on these streets, though it's a fine day in the summer. That's one thing that hasn't changed. She remembers how all the children stayed indoors with their parents. They walked around hunched, as if they carried a burden on their backs.

Later, Claudia would find out just what that burden was.

She stops in front of another empty house. Something about it disturbs her. Who used to live here? Then she remembers an old lady opening the door when she was wandering alone on the empty street, not sure what to do with herself. The lady invited her in and gave her biscuits, which looked plain but tasted rich and buttery. She let Claudia stroke her cat, which purred like a little machine and swished his tail in her face.

It is late afternoon turning into early evening, with the sun just showing signs of waning. The colours of houses here run to beige, olive and off-white, but these muted shades only seem to veil other hues that swirl and throb. Outlines between the houses, the sky, the ground and the trees around Erich's house are painfully sharp, yet bulge as if something strains against them. What will happen if they burst apart? She starts to feel dizzy, feels her breath catch again.

She's had that feeling before; it happened on a regular basis, but surely it isn't the time for it now . . .

It's so fucking quiet here. Even the sound of the sea is muffled.

When she was a kid, she always wanted to run about the streets and shout. She wanted to play games, listen to music. The only recreation for local children was swimming lessons, which she hated.

The windows at the community centre, the 'clubhouse,' are dark now.

But it was usually busy there. People used to do the ordinary things: play table tennis, work out in the gym. Sometimes they showed films. They could be old Humphrey Bogart films or recent blockbusters. Then something odd would turn up, films filled with dark thumping sounds, the rush of water and dissonant screeches.

And there was the pool, housed in the extension to the clubhouse. Its irregular shape didn't make sense for a public pool where people should just be swimming laps. It always had a dank smell to it. She remembers the constant sound of dripping and trickling, the bubbly under-water giggles from children as they tried to hold her head under the water in 'experiments' to see what happened to her woolly hair when it was soaked.

In this saline water, the children of Priory were also introduced to their religion. Charles Erich or Caitlin recited some rubbish before they dunked a kid under several times. Everyone went under then, not just Claudia.

How she hated the sight of Erich's man-boobs just above the water line. She's had nightmares about that, too. When she noticed such things, Erich used to glare at her and give a pincer-like twitch of his fingers as if he knew exactly what she was thinking. *"Do you have a question, Claudia?"*

It wasn't so bad when Lorraine came to give talks alongside Erich. She said that *our* fascinating entities (she never called them gods) used light and colour to communicate with each other, and they could speak to us that way if we worked to understand them.

"That's my mum," Claudia used to say. "That's my mum."

That was my mum, Claudia thinks as she turns left just after the community centre, and walks towards the house she used to share with Lorraine.

"Grief does strange things to people, and it turns them strange," Claudia's grandma Rita said. "I loved Lorraine when I first met her, and I still worry about her. But you won't ever go back to that place, will you?"

They were sitting around eating ginger cake in her grandparents' council flat near Portobello Road, a belated celebration for Claudia's twenty-fourth birthday just before she left for Priory. The windows were open, letting in the shouts of children and the smack of a ball against the ground. A familiar spasm of envy hits Claudia as she listened to the sounds of children playing.

The question came out of the blue, but Claudia had been pondering an answer since her arrival. "Mum asked me back for the summer," she said. "Says she needs help. She's my mum . . . Guess I'll try to help her."

"We wanted to do what we could for both of you when Carl died. But she cut us out when she took up with that cult. We're atheists and socialists and don't have time for any religion, much less one that worships sea serpents," snorted grandpa Joe.

"But my mum doesn't consider herself religious either," Claudia told them. "She joined those people in the name of science and scientific research."

"That's a funny way to be scientific," said Joe. "But at least you're here now. And you can always call this home."

Has she ever felt at home since her father's death? After years of hating her mother, Claudia tries to understand her actions. Perhaps that's why she's now here at Priory.

She remembers walking with Lorraine near the sea after it happened. Lorraine was explaining that her father had been in an accident while riding his bicycle to work. A very bad accident, which killed him.

Dying was something very old people did. Her granny, Lorraine's mother, died when she was a baby, but then her granny was very old. Her other grandparents, on her father's side, were old but not old enough to die.

The waves moved in and out along the shore, constant as a heartbeat.

Lorraine put her arm around Claudia and nodded towards the waves. "Does that make you feel calmer? It does that for me. That's why I study the sea. It's as mysterious as outer space. We know more about the moon than the sea on our own planet."

She spoke in a low soothing voice. "When I was a girl I watched it for hours. I was only watching the harbour in Liverpool. But my thoughts went beyond ships and commerce, to the great depths beyond the harbour. I knew then I wanted to learn more about that."

She talked about nature and time, and how every living thing must eventually die.

"But in the middle of this, we can love and create. There's always you and me. You're my girl and I'll always love you. And we'll always keep your father in our thoughts."

It sounded good at the time. Yet the next morning, having her father in her thoughts wasn't enough. She wanted to see him at breakfast, wanted to be with him. But one turn onto the wrong road, and a driver's miscalculation and carelessness, put an end to that.

And she knew having Dad in her thoughts wasn't enough for her mother, when she heard the stifled sobs through the night.

"Grief does strange things to people." So imagine life as a young woman, newly widowed, with a small child to bring up. Imagine if your dreams lay in ruins, and people who say they understand them and promise to fulfil them come along and 'help' you. And even if they hate who you are, they see there is knowledge to take from you.

Did the pull of Priory start with her father's death? Or had it been a bit of good news that brought her there, as much as the onslaught of the bad?

First, they had to move to a one-room flat. Lorraine was forced to jack in the oceanography course and work overtime as a lab assistant. Carl had been supporting

Lorraine in her studies, so he hadn't left any savings. And he'd been working at an IT start-up for a good freelance fee but no benefits, certainly not for widows.

Lorraine and Claudia went through their days half-asleep, trying not to feel much. At night they walked on the beach, while Lorraine told her tales of the sea and the creatures that lived in it. "Let the sound of the waves soothe you," Lorraine kept saying. Claudia tried.

At night they huddled together with the radio for company.

Then a prestigious science magazine accepted a paper Lorraine had submitted months ago. As Lorraine started to read her emails that morning, light from her computer screen showed up the grey tint to her skin, and all the new worry lines.

A sudden smile spread across it, driving the grey away.

"They want my paper! They're publishing my paper! I'd forgotten all about it . . . "

She hugged Claudia.

For a moment, Claudia thought such joy could only mean one thing: Her dad was coming back.

After that, Claudia still heard her mother crying at night, but there was less despair. She was grieving, but now she also had something to look forward to. Perhaps they both did.

When the article was published, it stirred up controversy. Claudia didn't understand what it was about, though Lorraine read some of the emails to her.

The article, Lorraine explained, was about bioluminescence and communication in deep sea creatures. There is no doubt they communicate with each other this way, but Lorraine speculated about how humans could read these signals. And perhaps there was much more to these creatures than we realised . . .

And then came an email from Mr Charles Erich at Priory, near Exham.

When she received Charles Erich's email, Lorraine stopped reading aloud, and frowned at the screen. "This man wants to talk about my article. And he has something he wants me to see . . . Maybe he's just a crazy guy. I've had a few of those contacting me."

"Maybe he *is* a crazy guy."

"But he seems to know what he's talking about, as if he's studied cephalopods himself."

"What's a cephalopod?"

"I'll tell you later, just let me reply to this email."

She should've said, *yes* he's crazy. Tell Mr Erich to fuck off.

But who'd listen to an eight-year-old kid?

Lorraine arranged to meet Mr Erich at a café near the Ocean Studies centre. She couldn't find a babysitter, so Claudia came along.

Lorraine fussed with her hair and her clothing, casual trousers and a loose top. To mark the occasion, she'd bought Claudia a new colouring book.

Young Claudia squirmed and shifted in the rock-hard chair. The bunches in her hair were too tight. Her scalp itched.

And Lorraine was wrong about the smart casual bit, because Mr Erich turned up in a suit and tie. He was tall and thin, with bright blue eyes and an erect posture. He was handsome in a gaunt and craggy way, like he could be an old movie star.

Though Lorraine was not petite by any means, she had to tip her head back to speak to the towering man as she shook his hand.

Claudia looked up from her colouring book, just in time to see the look of surprise pass over Mr Erich's face.

Young as she was, she'd seen this expression before.

Black. I didn't think she'd be black.

Claudia saw and knew this look, but Lorraine's mind was away with the sea creatures. Afterwards he barely registered Claudia's presence at all, as if Lorraine had taken her along as an accessory like a hat or a scarf.

And as he began to talk to Lorraine, polite interest replaced his surprise. This waxed into enthusiastic interest and fascination as the conversation progressed.

When they'd first moved to Priory, Claudia was afraid to go to the toilet on her own. She was convinced that a monster lived in the sewers beneath the house, glugging and sucking. She imagined its eyestalks rising out of the toilet like periscopes, getting a good look at her bottom.

Of course there's no monster, her mother told her. "Nothing is monstrous. There is only difference, and the unknown that we try to know. Life came from the sea, and its ancient creatures will help us understand the beginning of life and even the beginning of the world. Their thoughts have been unfathomable . . . until now."

Later, Lorraine placed her finger over her lips and led Claudia down a staircase, a tunnel, then more stairs. They entered a room that smelled of aromatic smoke mingled with earth and sea. Lorraine pulled a curtain back to display a scene that reminded Claudia of the underwater films her mother brought back from field trips. Was this a film, too? She felt like she was in a cinema. No, it's real, her mother said. This is a special window that shows us what's in the sea. Look. A pale green arm—no, a tentacle her mother called it— moved through the water. There was an expanse of something like skin. A huge eye filled the window, blinking. It looked almost human. Almost. An image was reflected in it, but Claudia couldn't see what it was.

Does it see us? A tentacle again, which began to glow with a blue light.

"Some might call this a colossal squid, but it's much more than that. It could be unique, and date back thousands and thousands of years . . . We've not even seen the whole of it. Isn't it beautiful?"

Young Claudia had to say yes. She had never seen a blue so pure.

Lorraine greets Claudia at the door. "I'm so glad you've returned to us. I missed you."

Claudia hugs her mother. Perhaps she's getting too thin . . . watch that she doesn't get like Erich. But she's still attractive, and once again Claudia wonders if her mother had ever dated anyone in all the years since her father had died.

But who the hell is *us?* Claudia pulls away. "I'm only here for a while. I have to return to my course, after all."

While Lorraine makes a pot of camomile tea—*piss*—Claudia looks around the house. She grew up here but it's still alien to her. When she was a teenager, only her posters of Jimi Hendrix and Poly Styrene in her room made her feel settled. She's glad she brought them back with her, along with a few gifts from her grandparents.

The white walls in the living room now boast paintings full of dark green and light, shafts of mysterious illumination and strong patterns of colour. Claudia reads an inscription on one painting in Lorraine's handwriting: *'In the vast water we rule. The water divides the worlds, and we drift through the divide.'*

We rule?

"I did those paintings," says Lorraine as she returns with the tea. "I've turned the garden shed into a studio and workshop. I started painting when I couldn't describe our creature's messages in words. It communicates in light and colour, so I tried to do that, too. People seem to like the paintings."

Claudia has to admit that they are striking pieces of art. How can something beautiful come from that creature?

But then, when she was a child she took pride in her mother's connection to the beast, especially when people gathered in the communion room to watch Lorraine swim up close to the creature and take pieces of it away.

MEAT, MOTION AND LIGHT

Before Claudia and her mother settled at Priory, collecting the communion meat had been dangerous. It was seen as another form of sacrifice. People volunteered for the task, anticipating honour after risk. Sometimes they survived, sometimes they didn't.

The creature only ate a sacrifice twice a year, so they harvested when the creature was sated, even sluggish. Someone went down, equipped in scuba gear, and cut some suckers off a tentacle.

The creature might only give a twitch. But even if it wasn't hungry, it could get annoyed. Then it would swat and maybe bite. Or give a quick slice with a talon capable of detaching the breathing apparatus, or rending the wetsuit and the flesh beneath it.

Lorraine, however, would descend in a specially designed diving bell that flashed coloured lights in a calculated sequence. It inspired a colourful display from the creature . . . and Lorraine's machine would 'luminesce' further in response.

Then she would emerge from her diving bell. As her slim form darted through the water, her balletic motions set off ripples of phosphorescence from the creature. Sometimes it sent out a warning red, but it always let her approach and remove a sucker, several of them. She would cup her prize in her hands, bow to the beast, then put her harvest in a rubber pouch slung across her waist.

Claudia enjoyed this display. When others taunted her, calling her 'nig-nog-landspawn' and other insults, she held her head high and retorted that her mother did an important job others were too scared to do.

Lorraine also worked at her desk on important tasks. She created colour charts and experimented with combinations that produced varied responses in the creature. She did further work on programs, algorithms and sequences to understand and articulate its messages. The creature perceived currents, any hint of disruption in the sea and seabed easily missed by humans, Lorraine had explained to Claudia. From this Lorraine compiled data, which was applied in a series of gambling manoeuvres, insurance scams and investments.

While it did not do so well on the crash of 2008, the creature did predict the tsunami of 2005. It sang of the levees breaking in New Orleans, of currents shifting and converging, of flooding in the UK and Europe in the years that followed.

And it called out again and again for blood and communion.

"Anyone can do this," Lorraine claimed, when it was time to get into her diving bell.

But no one did. Inevitably, the task fell upon Lorraine. And that was fine with her, since it brought her security and veneration in a most unlikely place.

Claudia excuses herself, saying she needs to unpack. She goes to her room and tries to relax within its magnolia walls, already missing her cramped little room in her shared house. Or Carl's old room in her grandparents' flat, now a study where she sometimes camps out among his ancient computers and 1990s albums.

The first thing she does is unroll her posters: Poly and Jimi. And her grandparents' presents . . . There's a portrait of her namesake, a civil rights leader called Claudia Jones, a copy of CLR James's *The Black Jacobins* and *Ain't I a Woman* by bell hooks . . . absolute classics missing from her education in the enclave.

She also has a photo of Kath banging away at her drums.

But she won't display Kath's photo here. She has to protect Kath, and keep her away from Priory in every way possible.

All these things belong to a world so distant from her now. That world has its dangers . . . police harassment, poverty, exploitative landlords. When she last visited her grandparents, they were in the throes of organising a meeting against council plans to sell part of their estate.

But whenever she settles in her father's old room for the night, she feels safe and so close to the young man her father had been, a shy geeky guy who also loved music. Being near the warmth and engagement of her grandparents always fills her with regret that she'd been snatched out of their world and thrust into Priory.

She listens to her iPod as she puts up her posters, playing Tamar-Kali's version of "Fire with Fire." As she sings along, she thinks about resuming her course in the autumn, ready to study what she chooses. Her plans to travel to the States next year, where she just might see Tamar live at the Afropunk Fest in Brooklyn.

This music represents *her* world, and she won't give it up.

And then she thinks about Kath, who must wonder where she is. She takes out her phone, ready to send a text message. But no, Kath would certainly want to join her. And she doesn't want Kath tainted with this place, or threatened by it.

Claudia closes her eyes. What would Kath think if she knew *everything*?

"I grew up in a religious community . . . a cult, really," Claudia once explained. "It was shit."

"Were they homophobic?"

Claudia had to laugh. "Not just homophobic. They'd be happy if sex didn't exist at all. They'd prefer it if women laid eggs and the guy came along and fertilised them, like fish. But my mother . . . she's a marine biologist, would probably say I'm wrong about the fish."

Kath shook her head, probably wondering what kind of marine biologist would join a cult.

My mum, that's who. And she'd been part of it, too. Only a kid, but she still played a part. Her mother had shown her the creature, the Nameless One with the silly name. *Isn't it beautiful?* She doesn't remember each time she saw it, not everything.

Then the *scenes* intrude, vivid fragments of them bobbing to the surface of her thoughts like turds . . . Turds coloured no doubt by *bioluminescence*, those memories that belong to the past turning into *now*.

Maybe she is nine, sitting at a table the size of a football pitch, the faces around it flushed. Where's her mother? Away on one of her trips. But Claudia is there with Mr and Mrs Links. Of the people she stayed with, they were the kindest. Maybe they were lonely because they didn't have any children.

Mrs Links puts food on Claudia's plate, a braised meat with potatoes and veg. Claudia lifts her fork to stab a chunk, but Mrs Links touches her wrist. "Not yet . . . This is a special meal, a rare treat, so we say something to express thanks. It's fine if you just listen."

People start chanting, their faces so serious it makes Claudia want to laugh. She doesn't know the words. She doesn't even know the language, but she does know she must never let herself laugh.

The taste of the meat is also new, very pungent and flavoursome. She likes it, as much as she dislikes everything else in the room. So she concentrates on flavours. The texture is fishlike, but solid. Like tuna steak perhaps, but better.

A stranger sits at the table, whose face she can't remember. He or she is only an undefined presence, soon to become an absence. There's a hole in her mind, soon filled with a whir of motion and struggle. Then they're down in the room with the window looking into the water.

A figure in a metal frame drops down, trailing bubbles from a scuba mask.

A tentacle extends and grasps the man. Mrs Links whispers in her ear.

What was in that whisper? Now, Claudia only recalls Lorraine's words on the beach after her father's accident: "All living things must die."

And if some must die sooner?

A slow glow suffuses the creature and a single light flickers within a sucker at the tip of the tentacle as it extends a slender probe. She remembers a word her mum used: *bioluminescence*.

And it skewers the man in the back . . .

She forgets what happens next. Maybe she wants to keep it that way.

But she knows what happened *afterwards*, when the creature had its fill.

The world tilts. Streams of light and fleeting, barely perceived images fill her mind. They taste of salt. They turn her tiny and terrified, but capable of seeing much more if she tried. Mrs Links holds her hand. "Breathe deep, dear. Isn't it incredible?"

"Good show, eh?" Mr Links beams at her.

The world turns tipsy, reality bleeding into a swirl of colour.

She felt a hint of this today as she walked down the street. Had the creature been feeding then?

Too soon, too soon. That was what Lorraine kept saying when she came back from her trip, and Claudia told her all about the dinner, the death and the tilt of the world. First she seemed upset with Mr and Mrs Links. Then she calmed down.

"It must've been frightening, but I hope you can see the wonder in it, too. Just imagine . . . the creature was letting you into another universe, or perhaps part of its world was pushing into ours. Deep in the sea, where the pressure is so immense, there may be *gaps*, and our creature swims through them. Its movements stir the sea and unsettle the world, and create passageways to other worlds that leak colours based on unknown forms of light. Some people call this phenomenon the 'impossible colours.'"

But what about the man, Claudia wanted to ask Lorraine. What was that white thing floating in the current? Had it been a bone?

It must've been frightening. So had she been scared, a little girl watching a man get eaten?

As they filed up those stairs she'd been blinking,

determined not to cry. Crying only brought punishment and pain.

"Do you have any questions?" A familiar voice beside her made her jump.

Mr Erich . . . Where did he come from? Perhaps he'd made himself invisible in a corner somewhere, or slithered in through a crack in the wall.

"Claudia, do you see now that everything has its price?" Erich gave her his thin-lipped smile. "The meat anchors the Nameless One in our world. Then it gives us visions that bring wisdom, and provides information that brings us prosperity. But all of that must be paid for."

Lorraine calls Claudia to dinner. She is relieved that it's not seafood, but vegetable lasagne with spinach and red beans, spiced to give a bit of a kick.

"Now, Claudia . . . there's a meeting at the community centre. You'll find out what's happening there. And remember, even though you've been away you can still vote."

The lasagne starts to lose its flavour as that familiar churning starts up in her stomach. "Is that why you asked me here, so I can vote for you? And since when did we vote on anything around here? We only show hands to rubber-stamp the dictates of Charles Erich!"

She was really hoping to avoid Charles Erich during her stay. And now she's been railroaded into a meeting.

"Like I said, things have changed since you were

last here," Lorraine replies. "Charles is getting old, after all. And our creature is getting very moody, and I have some ideas why."

"I can hardly wait to find out."

Lorraine doesn't respond, but excuses herself to get ready.

After dinner they make their way to the centre. Outside, Claudia feels dizzy again as people emerge from their houses. Though the street is full, there's little conversation or animation as people move towards their destination.

Inside, the building is crowded. Folding seats have been added to the usual heavy oak chairs. There is a hush as Charles Erich assumes his place at a podium, flanked by members of the Committee. Self-satisfied pompous Tory gits . . . Losing on the chapel must've taken them down a peg or two, but that's obviously not enough. She struggles against an urge to suck her teeth at them, a gesture she only learned after she left home.

Erich calls the meeting to order, his voice deep and resonant as he recites an invocation. Words ring out in the language that Claudia never wanted to learn, though some kids studied it and made up swear words.

Though Erich's voice is just as strong, the rest of his physical being seems diminished. Like everything else here, like the boarded-up house.

He talks about funding and recruiting, about dues to be paid by high-profile members of the community and extracted from those whose profiles are lower.

MEAT, MOTION AND LIGHT

Claudia is not interested in these things, and looks about the room. She thinks her ex-boyfriend Roddy, if you can call him that, would not welcome the idea that she's now queer. She tries to catch his eye though, but he's sitting with his arms folded and eyes trained straight ahead on Erich. His Clash-loving sister Theresa, what her mum would have called her 'bezzie' in the old days, is sitting behind him.

Claudia eyes the spiralling lines of scars down the neck of a suave-looking man a few rows in front of her. Their pattern widens, then disappears under his shirt. He is flanked by a bejewelled woman, who sports bare arms showing the signs of deep gouging. What happened to them?

"As you know, we experienced a setback when we tried to take our chapel out of the public realm and extend the boundaries of our community," Erich is saying.

"Now our position has been vindicated by recent events . . . The chapel has been vandalised!" The expected gasp comes from the front row, but the response from the rest of the room is muted. Erich pauses, awaiting the expected reaction. A flicker of confusion crosses his face when it doesn't come, then he glances at his notes and clears his throat. "This is what happens when such an important place is open to just anyone. People with no understanding will defile it.

"So we will look again at this absurd backtracking on our government's promise to put state property on the open market. There are loopholes—legal and otherwise—we can identify and use to our advantage."

Erich looks in Claudia's direction as he discusses

'loopholes.' That gaze again, as if he can read her mind. Of course he can't; he's only human. But he has the ability to make people believe he's more than that. She certainly believed when she was little.

Will he call on her to talk about the law and that stupid chapel? She's only a student. And this isn't the time or place to announce that she's about to change her speciality from property law to human rights.

There's a tremor in Erich's right hand. Barbara the banker has a tired downward drag to her hooded eyes, and her lean husband Harvey has run to flab and paunch. Those shots of super-squid ink haven't proved to be the elixir of youth, after all. Erich, and all those others who terrified her as a child, now seem shrunken or ridiculous.

In contrast, Lorraine is resplendent in an orange and purple hair wrap, make-up immaculate, and a long filmy dress the same green as the sea. Others surround her, casting admiring glances. Mum definitely has a following here. Her old babysitters, Harry and Lana Link, are among Lorraine's fans. Lana looks at Claudia and pats a seat near her, but Claudia shakes her head. She's sitting closest to the door.

After a pause in the proceedings, Erich suggests moving on. A stirring passes through the room.

"And now, we need to talk about a crucial matter. The Nameless One has refused a sacrifice."

There is a gasp from the front row, but it seems rather perfunctory. Perhaps this particular moggie has been out of the bag for a long time.

"Our creature is restless. It is still hungry. We have a crisis on our hands."

Now Lorraine gets up, faces the audience and

makes a wide queenly gesture with her arms. "Fellow worshippers and adepts, Brother Charles speaks of a crisis, but I proclaim that we have a *breakthrough* on our horizon!"

No one, just no one would have dared to interrupt Charles Erich back in the days when she lived here. Dreadful punishment would have resulted. Claudia eyes the scars on the couple a few rows in front of her.

Lorraine's supporters stand up and clap, while Erich's lot are more restrained in expressing their displeasure. Despite all the other changes, old Harvey Philips still has the same expression on his face—as if he's caught a whiff of something rotten. It must come from all those years of sniffing Erich's farts.

"Your mother's wonderful," a woman whispers to Claudia. "You people have such a good grasp of magic and nature. I really envy your heritage."

Envy away, lady. How much heritage did I get, stuck here with the likes of you?

So what has changed, now that some of these people look at Lorraine with adoration instead of shock that she has entered their lily-white abode? Not much. They now put her mother on a pedestal, render her exotic as the black earth mother or sea mother who has the ear of the god. They regard her as a shaman . . . but Claudia suspects shamans can be expendable if they don't perform.

"Nonsense," shouts Roddy, Claudia's now respectable ex. "Breakthrough, you say? This behaviour just means the creature's hungry. We must give it additional sacrifices. And let's face it, the last one was below par."

"That's my son you're talking about!" The scarred

man stands. "Since when did we use members of our community for sacrifices? Yes, by all means send runaways down, but my son did not run away. He was committed to this community. Sure, he was high-spirited sometimes . . ."

"Your son was a pest and a nuisance," retorts Erich. "Yet obviously not suitable for sacrifice. We should move the date forward for the next one, and offer two tributes . . ."

Nauseous dread strikes at Claudia. Is this why her mother insisted she return? But no . . . it's been said that the creature only eats 'white meat.' She overheard that years ago when Barbara was discussing a prospective victim with her husband.

Back in RE class, Erich once said in a lecture: "When our ancestors crawled out of the sea, their flesh was pure and white, unsullied by toil and light. And labour on the surface of the world toughened and browned human skin."

Then Lorraine argued against that on a scientific basis; obviously not all sea creatures are *white*.

Shut up, Mum. Claudia had been thinking at the time. *Just shut up.*

But now Claudia is cheering her mother on as she claims the floor again. "What happened at the last sacrifice matters less than what is happening now. How many of us have actually observed the changes in the Nameless One? It's sending out luminescent signals constantly, the planes bend frequently. We can all feel it. I suggest we all go down and look at the evidence."

Clapping greets this suggestion. Erich looks around the room with growing panic, like a cornered animal. He confers with his minions, who don't seem too happy either. Caitlin is looking down with a furrowed brow as she spins her bangles around her wrist again and again; Barbara's face is turning a blotchy red.

But cornered animals can be doubly dangerous, even when they're outnumbered. Claudia glances at pockets and belts, but sees no obvious firearms or weapons. Perhaps Erich has counted on forcing obedience in other ways.

Ignoring the group at the front, most people in the room begin to make their way down the stairs into the earth. Old feelings wash through Claudia as she descends the twisting stairs along with them. The filthiest kind of fear, fear that is infected by guilt.

Claudia remembers the grinning girl who sneaked into the chapel during that long-ago RE session. The stranger seemed to shine, though her face was smudged and she was actually quite dirty. But compared with Priory children, she radiated life and energy as she giggled silently in the back. When she met Claudia's glance, she moved forward and tentatively poked her with her finger.

Claudia fell immediately in love.

"Get that child out of here," teacher Caitlin commanded.

The girl fled before anyone made a move. But Claudia found her later, hiding in the bushes and staring at the carving.

"D'you like that? I know where the *real* creature is. My mum showed me and I can show you."

And now Lorraine is opening the curtains over the same window with a flourish. Yes, the Nameless One with the silly name is doing its thing.

The teeth and probes at the centre of the creature's

suckers glow, transformed into hundreds of stars. They are the pure green of an emerald flame, an 'impossible colour' that casts its light into hidden parts of her mind.

"Bioluminescence. Remember? Deep sea creatures have to make their own light because they survive in total darkness. But our creature has never emitted luminescence in this way before. It hasn't needed to. Creatures shine to hunt, to communicate—as it communicates with us after we feed it—or to attract mates."

"It doesn't need to hunt here. We feed it. It's been domesticated," suggests Claudia.

People turn around to look at her, and Claudia wants to cringe. Then she sees signs of respect on a few faces, as if she's been touched with the same glittering brush that has been extended to her mother.

"Yes, it usually displays a rather mild luminescence," Lorraine replies. "But no more. Each day it grows brighter and more elaborate."

Concentric rings of colour radiate through of its body, travelling down its tentacles and up again. They shift through the spectrum, then throb into purple and magenta and cool into green again. It gives Claudia a bubbly feeling to watch it.

"Our creature is agitated, it's trying to communicate. But I don't think it's communicating with us."

"I know what it is saying. It hasn't eaten enough. The last sacrifice was unsuitable, some scrawny teenager it swatted aside," says Erich.

"You bastard!" The boy's father is trying to get to Erich, ready to take a swing. But Lorraine lays a restraining hand on his arm. "*Don't*, that's not the way."

Claudia asks: "Did you say it flashes the lights to attract mates?"

"Exactly. Look at the beauty of those colours, those signals. That is hardly a complaint. You think it is signalling hunger. And you may be right. But it's hunger of a different kind. You don't need to know the coding and the tables of interpretation to guess. Those are the colours and pulsations of celebration . . . of desire. It's seeking a mate. Perhaps one is approaching. This is a wonderful event."

"It's in love then, and pining?" Claudia means to be sarcastic but a collective 'awwww' sounds throughout the room.

Erich looks as if the steel poker he carries up his arse has been given a few more pushes upwards. "How can there be another? We looked everywhere. *You* looked everywhere."

Yes, Claudia remembers those trips. Terrible times for her. When her mother went on voyages for weeks at a time, she'd stay with other families where she was often ignored or bullied. Even the cuddly Links did the wrong things and made her feel strange.

"I can't answer that question now, though we may be able to answer that soon. But I do know one thing for sure. Our Nameless One's mate will arrive. And let's be prepared, let's welcome it and learn from it."

Every night, people gather in the underground chamber to watch the light show and wait for the creature's mate to arrive. Some nights they're silent, other times they chant and pray. Claudia doesn't see how that will help Sucker-mucker pull, but these people have faith. Lorraine's so certain, her confidence unshakeable.

Even Charles Erich joins the assembly, Caitlin by his side. She offers her own pronouncements on the creature's signals, but she doesn't get it the way Lorraine does.

During the day Lorraine spends most of her time in her garden workshop. Mechanical and grinding sounds come from the shed.

Claudia gets bored during the afternoons, and still doesn't feel entirely like herself. She tries to study for next term, and read her grandparents' birthday books. She sends vague text messages to Kath. She misses her, but doesn't want to encourage her to come to Priory. She wants to get out of this place and see her. She wants to play with the band again. What power does Erich hold over her now? Her mother could leave, too, and get a job at a university.

But she feels rooted, as if sucked down in quick sand. She wants to see what happens next. What if the monster's mate doesn't arrive? For her mother's sake, she hopes it does. She finds herself yearning for the mate to appear, for this change to take place. Given the creature's current behaviour, it might end the sacrifices. Maybe they'll both swim out to the deep sea where they belong.

She joins the others to watch the lights coil and burst from within the creature. The rhythm of the lights pounds in her ears. She feels disconnected, as if the light flowing through her leaves a different substance in its wake. But then her body feels much more present, expanding beyond its boundaries.

Lorraine puts her hand across Claudia's forehead as if she's a child again, getting checked out for fever. "What is it? Are you feeling the lights within you?"

"Dunno about that. Just weird. I think I want to go home. Back to London."

Claudia has been saying that every night.

"I know it gets intense," says Lorraine. "After all, it uses those signals to attract prey or mates, so any living creature can be affected . . . some more than others. I'm working on a way to filter the signals so we can keep our wits. We might indeed need to lose them in order to traverse the dimensions, but this might not be the time or place."

Claudia imagines these *wits* bursting out of someone's belly and trailing behind as they cross the space between dimensions, tight coils of consciousness unravelling.

Meanwhile, the enclave bubbles and ferments, while the shouty meetings get less turbulent now Erich and his supporters have decided to play along.

Claudia—and Lorraine—know very well that the old guard is waiting in the wings for failure. How long will peoples' patience last?

The creature continues to entrance its audience with sinuous movements of its tentacles, weaving strands of light from unknown spectrums. Its suckers swell to let loose fountains of sparks.

"What is it saying, Lorraine?"

Lorraine closes her eyes and intones an interpretation. It all sounds like New Age bollocks.

Then Claudia speaks up. "Have we forgotten that our friend is on the pull and it must absolutely have its mate? I mean, what's eating people compared to a shag with a fellow squid?" With that, she bursts into a chorus of "Looking for Love," Afropunk style, Poly Styrene meeting Gloria Gaynor or Donna Summer or whoever sings that song.

The scarred couple claps, mouths stretched in glassy smiles. Barbara gives an incongruous and rather ghastly *yip* of encouragement. Others carry on clapping. Do they think this will draw in their god's consort? All those flashing lights must have gone to their head, Claudia thinks. And maybe that's all for the best.

She keeps singing. With no band behind her, she just belts out everything she knows. Romance plays an important part in the content, but eventually she runs out of romantic numbers. She's left with her favourite, "Fire with Fire."

Claudia could swear that the creature's colour brightens in response. And then it changes, the green darkening to near-black. Can it even hear her? She has no idea how her noise carries through the glass of the window, which seems to bend and waver. She doesn't know if her voice would carry at all through the water.

And why is she singing to this vast human-eating creature? Is she becoming her mother, who dragged her into this cult? Now she's an adult, participating in it, playing the role of minstrel rather than singing what is true to her heart.

MEAT, MOTION AND LIGHT

One evening the creature moves past the window, and its eye suddenly fills it. Claudia now sees what is contained within the upper layer of that eye. It is too late to turn away from it now.

The creature must hoard these images . . . the faces and even the thoughts of those it consumes. That's why it demands more than fish and aquatic mammals; it eats and savours human minds, 'souls' as well as flesh.

In her recurring dreams she can't bear to look in that eye. She always wakes up before she sees the face trapped within it.

But now she sees it. She sees the girl who came to play with her years ago, a glimmer against the black hole of the creature's pupil.

At the time she was so happy to be making a friend in a place where she had no friends. Now she could impress her new playmate with the secret at the heart of her community.

She took the girl down to the room that her mother had shown her. She remembered how to turn on the lights and open the curtains to reveal the creature.

"You didn't believe me, but this is the monster on the wall of the chapel. Except it's a god. And my mother is learning how to talk to it. Well, maybe it's not God. But it's pretty cool. We don't see the whole thing 'cause it's so big, but it fits itself into this big watery chamber or . . . well something like that. And it changes colours and shines. That's how it talks."

Then Caitlin walked in. *Get this child out of here,* Caitlin had demanded in the chapel. But this time she didn't shout. Her eyes gleamed at the centre of her spidery false eyelashes, then she smiled. "Who are you?"

When the girl said she came from the children's home on the other side of Exham and no one minded if she's gone and she liked it better at Priory, Caitlin smiled even more. "Did you enjoy your visit? Would you like to stay for dinner?"

Claudia stops singing. This memory has been lying in wait for her all along. Now it hits her like a blow to the stomach. What an idiot she must be, *singing* to these people and to this thing.

It doesn't matter, though. Because the creature is moving and stretching its tentacles as if reaching for something bigger than itself. Its eye is still turned towards the window but it looks far beyond it, and its surface now reflects nothing human. It opens its beak and extends an iridescent orange tongue. And then another limb begins to extend from its body. It is thicker than a tentacle, becoming longer.

It's a massive erection.

Word must have got out, because everyone in Priory descends into the communion room. It's crowded and hot as they turn their gaze onto the creature in the window, which has taken on a rippling blood-red glow. It opens its suckers; stars at their centres wink suggestively.

Claudia sees Nigel the security guy sneaking down the stairs. Nigel and his co-workers have never been invited to these affairs, but she gives him a discreet nod.

As the creature moves its tentacles through the water, more tentacles snake in through the gaps. These tangle and tease and twine, suckers opening like morning glories with needle stamens. They make a ripping motion, and a massive bulk funnels through the spaces between the limbs of the Nameless One. The room lurches and water gurgles in the pipes.

Then there are two creatures, glowing and rending. The window bends inwards towards the room to accommodate the newcomer. Claudia draws back with everyone else, afraid the sea will burst out of the glass. But the surfaces stretch to embrace the new dimensions.

This newcomer extends its claws, opens and contracts its suckers. The two arc towards each other and clamp on.

"Man . . . look at the size of that schlong! Like a submarine!" Nigel bellows.

Stunned silence greets this comment, though Claudia chuckles.

"What are you doing here?" Charles Erich hisses at him. "Why aren't you at your station?" For a moment, Erich seems his old self. His back is ramrod straight. He looks down from his height, still expecting to be obeyed with the same certainty that each breath will be followed by another.

But Nigel ignores him, and winks at Claudia and Lorraine. "But like an old song goes . . . *it ain't the meat, it's the motion.*"

This time Claudia isn't the only one who laughs.

Lorraine smiles at Nigel. "Yes, the giant squid and its colossal cousin are known to have penises that extend almost as long as its body when erect . . . "

Charles Erich still glowers at the impudent Nigel, but his glare is glazing and unfocusing as the creatures reach for each other, circle around, retreat and advance. Their lights flicker in ever-changing patterns, on and off. Claudia has to see the next change in the pattern.

While explaining these facts Lorraine places herself right in the light, the bioluminescence flickering over her face as she extends her arms to illustrate her point. *Almost* as long as its body?

"Mum, didn't you say the creature inhabits more than one dimension? So that means that it's . . . " Then Claudia's not really sure what that means, as the creature's light sifts through her vision, penetrates her brain. The colours leach into everything she sees, tainting her sensations, too.

Desire aches and hurts and lights her up. She can't see beyond the satisfaction of this ache. Ages have passed her by in a state of sleep. Now she's awake to her purpose.

Time dilates. Currents caress her. Skin lights pulsate, inviting entry. She spreads her arms, ready to embrace . . . everything. Or Nigel?

"Claudia! Put these goggles on! I've just put on mine."

"Why? I want to see. Don't you want to? That's what you brought me here for!"

"Put the fucking glasses on. You're being drawn in . . . Look away from the window, at the room."

Now gatekeeper Nigel is swooning in the arms of Barbara the banker, while none other than Roddy hauls off Harvey's trousers and lands a bite on a buttock, leaving a wide red mark. The Links are going for it in a threesome with the quiet retiree who runs the community centre, while Charles Erich and consort Caitlin entwine in front of the window. They seem to twist and dance among the vivid entrails of the mating creatures.

The male breaks the female's skin, ejecting streams that collect in puddles beneath it.

She claws at his organ, winds her tentacles around it, her own star-glow suckers squeezing and rending.

The points of light in his claws are as distant as real stars, shining from light years away. They open and close. Ripping pain, wild pleasure. There's a shout and blood splatters onto the parquet floor. It must be . . .

A pair of goggles gets shoved over Claudia's head. "Don't take them off," Lorraine says near Claudia's ear. "You need to stay sensible. We're recording everything. We can watch and study and immerse later . . . Erich has his agenda. He's turning into an old fool, but don't underestimate him!"

Glasses or not, Claudia is transfixed. The others are possessed; perhaps there's a difference. They thrash and mingle with each other as the lights bathe them.

The female's wounds widen, sucking in the male's

claws. She opens her beak and her mouth expands and draws more of him in. He bleeds radiant fluid in gushes.

Their parts twist around each other, guts quiver crimson. Suckers clash and clasp as another rush coats the female. She is still, then she pushes out streams of glowing ovals, tumbling over each other.

Eggs.

Nigel gazes over Barbara's head and lets out a whistle. "That's a lot of taramasalata going on there."

The two creatures continue to clasp each other, but their movements begin to slow. Another hole appears in the male's side, revealing a quivering shape that contracts and flares like a bellows.

Each creature heaves, spreading itself out further.

The colours pale. The monsters shake and go still, leaving only the pearly shine of the eggs.

When Claudia takes off her goggles, the world itself has also turned pale and the eggs begin to drift away with the current.

She hears a bewildered intake of breath all around her, followed by groans and whimpers. What happened to us? What happened to him? What happened to *her*? It's not moving. Is it . . . he . . . she . . . *dead*? Both of them.

"Too right!" proclaims Claudia. "Your god is dead, and so's his bitch!"

It's over? The whispers continue. Roddy bangs on the window, as if it could wake up the creatures. "No, no, you can't leave us!"

Nigel gets his phone out and begins taking photos.

Then there's sobbing, quiet at first. It grows louder and fills the room, a familiar sound to Claudia. She heard it many times after her father died. Lorraine crying at night, trying to hide her grief from her daughter, but not succeeding.

Lorraine doesn't try to disguise her grief now. The sobs catch and snarl, heartbroken.

Claudia puts her arm around Lorraine. "Come on, Mum, we have to go. Leave those arseholes in the wreckage, stuck with their dead gods."

"He will rise," Erich mutters from a kneeling position. This is echoed by Harvey Philips as he struggles to pull his trousers up.

"Shut the fuck up!" Claudia lands a kick at Erich.

A mere glance from this man used to terrify her. He doesn't frighten her now. As her foot connects, his body feels light and frail. And still, he barely notices as he continues to intone his nonsense.

She hears enraged shouting behind her. His henchmen? She could certainly deal with Mr Philips, even if he's managed to get his pants up. But the others?

"Too easy! Too easy . . . " Someone grabs Claudia's shoulder.

Claudia turns to face the father of the sacrificed boy, the scarred man.

"A kick! Is that all you're giving that murdering bastard? You're letting him off too easy. I'll show him much more than that . . . " The man pushes past her. He lands a few of his own kicks, then he starts to bang Erich's head against the floor. More blood begins to spatter. Claudia dodges out of the way, and grabs her mother.

"C'mon, let's go. You don't want to stay here with this lot of nutters now. Maybe they helped you in the past and you got to play with their pet, but it's dead.

It's over. Get a life, you and me both. Come on . . . I know where we can stay. We'll go to grandma and grandpa's first . . . "

"He will rise," Caitlin insists in a shrill voice as she tries to adjust her ripped dress. "He *will* rise."

"Oh no he won't," sighs Lorraine. "Giant and colossal squids die after mating. Or that's the hypothesis. It's not been proven for all species."

"Well, look at that." Claudia gestures to the window. "Dead as fucking dodos. We have the proof in front of us. Let's go." She tugs at Lorraine's arm.

Lorraine only looks out the window to the sea and sobs again. She goes up to the window and runs her hand over the glass, trying to touch the remains of the creatures. She finally lingers over an egg. A wave pushes more eggs out of view.

"It's done. The gods are dead. Mum, I have to go." She waits a minute, hoping that Lorraine will say, 'I'll come, too.' But she's still gazing at those goddamn eggs, tears running down her face. It makes Claudia want to cry, too. But she doesn't have time for that. If Lorraine won't leave this place, she can't force her.

"You know where to find me," Claudia says at last.

The room still rumbles with confusion. Caitlin insists again that he will rise; Philips joins in and a ragged chant gets going, while others join Lorraine's keening. But Claudia turns her back on all that, and starts to climb the winding staircase. As she gets to the top, she thinks she hears laughter and shouting. But who could be laughing now?

And when she stands in the sunlight at the open door, she understands she didn't imagine those voices. A cooling breeze carries them, and Claudia follows the sound towards the gate of Priory. For a moment she feels the old pang that came when she heard young people at play, laughter at a distance too far for her to cross. But this time she does make the crossing, down the road.

The kids must have disabled the electric fence while Nigel enjoyed the show, because they're now pounding and hacking and pulling the whole thing down. Roberta waves.

Claudia rushes over to help.

AFTERWORD BY THE EDITOR/PUBLISHER

**ND SO THEIR** stories come to an end ...

Or do they?

Isn't an ending nothing more than a major change? A change in the lives of all these characters? And although the stories in this collection seem fantastical, the basic premises have happened repeatedly throughout history—in different ways, of course, but the world's history is based on making others feel like outsiders. If you don't understand something, push it away!

There are certain benefits to calling others outsiders. When they're the outsiders, we're not. But eventually, in seeking the differences in others so we can feel special, we end up alone and as outsiders yet again.

Did Charles Erich not start Priory so he could feel like less of an outsider? Now his life has come full circle, and he's on the outside again. Has he been defeated, or will he find another way to fit in? What will happen to his constituents? Will Harvey Philips ever be in charge outside his actual office? Or will his empire crumble now that Priory is obsolete. Will any of them ever fit in again?

Who knows, perhaps some of them are living right down your block, no longer hiding behind high walls. Who needs high walls when everyone thinks you're just a normal neighbour? Makes you wonder what your neighbours are up to when there are so many cars parked out front. Perhaps a friendly dinner followed by tea and rituals below. Hell, there might be a catacomb below your house right now.

That's the beauty of Lovecraft's work. Those unknown yet hinted subtleties in Lovecraft's "The Outsider" that make it so fascinating. He's showing us the tip of the pyramid above the Sahara, allowing our imagination to fill in the rest. And who knows your own fears better than *you*?

This book has also been a personal journey for me. My original short story idea of Priory birthed this project. I believe the name is "For Those Below," and perhaps some day I'll finish it. I was about 10,000 words into the planned 15,000 word story, when the lonesomeness of the solitary author struck.

Similar to as authors like Robert E. Howard contributing to the Lovecraft mythos, I realised I needed to expand on my idea with the input of other authors. I wondered what they'd do with these characters. And strangely enough, stepping into the role of publisher and editor made me feel like less of an outsider, and I hope the authors felt that same bond with one another. This one idea turned into hundreds of emails between our group. So just like any cult or movement out there, a legend can be created from just an idea. Hell, that's where Crystal Lake Publishing began.

There are of course a lot of racial issues behind the legacy of H.P. Lovecraft. Living in South Africa I know exactly what people are capable of doing to each other—call it racism, xenophobia, or attempted genocide. "But will they, or anyone on this planet, become enlightened, like a lot of true fans believe Lovecraft did, and cast aside prejudice for truth?" Something to that effect so that you appear, as publisher, to be an authority on Lovecraft and truly coalesce his legacy—and enlightenment—with everyone else's? All I know is we're all readers here, fans of Dark Fiction, Horror, Sci-fi, Fantasy, Thrillers—call it what you will. And I don't care if you're pink, purple, or green, you're all pretty damn cool in my book.

Like Lovecraft's latter years, we're the open minded—those not just venturing outside the box but living there. The self-educated. With our own opinions. Those who've read enough books to know the difference between right and wrong, good and evil.

So people tend to call us The Outsiders, since they don't understand us. Their loss.

Joe Mynhardt
20 April, 2015

AUTHOR BIOGRAPHIES

Stephen Bacon's fiction has been published in *Cemetery Dance*, *Black Static*, *Shadows & Tall Trees*, *Crimewave*, *Terror Tales of Yorkshire*, *Murmurations*, and has been selected for *Best Horror of the Year*. He had stories in *Fear the Reaper* and *For the Night Is Dark*, both from Crystal Lake Publishing. His debut collection, *Peel Back the Sky* was published by Gray Friar Press.

James Everington mainly writes dark, supernatural fiction, although he occasionally takes a break and writes dark, non-supernatural fiction. His second collection of such tales, *Falling Over*, is out now from Infinity Plus. A monthly serial, *The Quarantined City*, is being released during 2015 from Spectral Press and he has stories forthcoming from *Supernatural Tales*, Fox Spirit, and Knightwatch Press.

He has a black cat and cream carpets, which shows how much thought he puts into those parts of his life that aren't book-related.

Oh and he drinks Guinness, if anyone's asking. You can find out what James is currently up to at his Scattershot Writing site.

Gary Fry lives in Dracula's Whitby, literally around the corner from where Bram Stoker was staying while thinking about that legendary character. Gary has a PhD in psychology, but his first love is literature. He was the first author in PS Publishing's Showcase series, and none other than Ramsey Campbell has described him as "*a master.*" He is the author of more than 100 published short stories and 15 books, including novels, novellas and collections. His latest are the Lovecraftian novel *Conjure House* (DarkFuse, 2013); the short story collection *Shades of Nothingness* (PS Publishing, 2013); the original zombie novel *Severed*, and novellas *Menace, Savage* and *Mutator* (DarkFuse, 2014). Gary warmly welcomes all to his web presence: www.gary-fry.comwww.gary-fry.com

V. H. Leslie's stories have appeared in *Black Static, Interzone, Weird Fiction Review, Strange Tales IV, Best British Horror* and *Best British Fantasy*. She has also had fiction and non-fiction published in *Shadows and Tall Trees* and is a columnist for *This is Horror*. She was recently awarded a Hawthornden Fellowship and the Lightship First Chapter Prize. 2015 will see the release of her novella 'Bodies of Water' as part of the Remains series from Salt Publishing and her debut short story collection *Skein and Bone* from Undertow Books. More information on the author can be found at www.vhleslie.wordpress.com

Joe Mynhardt is a South African horror writer, publisher, editor and teacher.

Joe is the owner of Crystal Lake Publishing, which he started in August, 2012. He has published and edited short stories, novellas, interviews and essays by the likes of Ramsey Campbell, Jack Ketchum, Graham Masterton, John Carpenter, Adam Nevill, Lisa Morton, Elizabeth Massie, Joe McKinney, Edward Lee, Wes Craven, John Carpenter, George A. Romero, Mick Garris, and hundreds more.

Crystal Lake Publishing believes in reaching out to all authors, new and experienced, and being a beacon of friendship and guidance in the Dark Fiction field.

You can read more about Joe and Crystal Lake Publishing at www.crystallakepub.com or find him on Facebook."

Joe is also an Associate member of the HWA.

Rosanne Rabinowitz got hooked on writing when she helped produce 'zines in the 1990s such as *Feminaxe* and *Bad Attitude,* contributing articles, reviews and interviews. Then she began to make stuff up . . . Her fiction has since found its way to journals like *Postscripts* and *Black Static* and her novella, *Helen's Story,* has received a Shirley Jackson Award nomination for achievement in the 'literature of the dark fantastic.'

Other work in print includes contributions to *Never Again: Weird Fiction Against Racism and Fascism* and another novella in the award-winning anthology *Extended Play: the Elastic Book of Music,* plus recent entries in *Horror Uncut* and *Jews vs Aliens.* Future releases include stories in *Tales from the Vatican Vaults* and *Soliliquy for Pan.* She occasionally writes non-fiction for union, community and campaign websites.

Rosanne lives in South London, so it's no surprise that her contribution to the anthology *Horror Without Victims* is titled "Lambeth North." She is a graduate of the Sheffield Hallam University MA in Writing.

For more information visit: rosannerabinowitz.wordpress.com

OTHER CRYSTAL LAKE PUBLISHING ANTHOLOGIES:

TALES FROM THE LAKE VOL.1—Edited by Joe Mynhardt

Dive into fourteen tales of non-themed horror, with short stories and dark poems by some of the best horror writers in the world, including a story by the master himself, Graham Masterton.

Allow the very first instalment of Tales From the Lake to transport you to lakeside terror in *Lover, Come Back to Me*, *Lady of Lost Lake*, and *Game On*; journey to the basement of your local pet store in *Dead Pull* and your neighbourhood pub in *O'Halloran's*; visit the apocalypse in *Devil's Night*; travel to Africa in *Witch-Compass* and *The Reunion*; spend time with talking dolls in *Don't Look at Me*; experience the horrors of drug addiction from close up in *Junksick*; and climb a ladder to the heavens in *Perrollo's Ladder*.

Tales From the Lake Vol.1 includes the winning stories from the 2013 Tales From the Lake Horror Writing Competition: a nautical tale in Jenn Loring's *The Art of Wrecking*; a bizarre story of strange addictions in J. Daniel Stone's *Alternative Muses*; and a cult horror story in the jungles of South America in William Ritchey's *Las Maquinas*.

Line-up: Graham Masterton, G.N Braun, Taylor Grant, John Palisano, Charles Day, John Paul Allen,

Bev Vincent, Elizabeth Massie, Joan De La Haye, Tim Curran, Tim Waggoner, Jennifer Loring, J. Daniel Stone, William Ritchey and Blaze McRob.

Introduction by Rocky Wood—president of the HWA.

Artwork by award winning artist Ben Baldwin.

Tales from The Lake Vol.1 is available from Amazon: http://getbook.at/AmazonLakeVOne

FEAR THE REAPER—Edited by Joe Mynhardt

A horror anthology about Death and the Grim Reaper.

Includes stories by Rick Hautala, Taylor Grant, Joe McKinney, Gary Fry, Ross Warren, Marty Young, Stephen Bacon, Dean M Drinkel, Richard Thomas, Sam Stone, Eric S Brown, Mark Sheldon, Steve Lockley, Robert S. Wilson, Jeremy C Shipp, Jeff Strand, Lawrence Santoro, E.C. McMullen Jr., Rena Mason, John Kenny and Gary A. Braunbeck.

Includes a poem by Adam Lowe, an introduction by Gary McMahon and a cover by Ben Baldwin.

Interior artwork by Will Jacques.

Artwork by award winning artist Ben Baldwin.

Fear the Reaper is available from Amazon: http://myBook.to/fearthereaper

FOR THE NIGHT IS DARK—Edited by Ross Warren

A horror anthology about the fear of the dark, and that which hides within.

Stories by Gary McMahon, William Meikle, Jasper Bark, Jeremy C Shipp, Robert W. Walker, Stephen Bacon, Mark West, Scott Nicholson, Tonia Brown, G. N. Braun, Blaze McRob, Benedict J. Jones, Daniel I. Russell, Kevin Lucia, Tracie Mcbride, Armand Rosamilia, John Claude Smith, Ray Cluley, Carole Johnstone, and Joe Mynhardt.

Artwork by award winning artist Ben Baldwin.

For the Night is Dark is available from Amazon: http://mybook.to/ForTheNightIsDark

Connect with Crystal Lake Publishing

Website (be sure to sign up for our newsletter):
www.crystallakepub.com
Facebook:
www.facebook.com/Crystallakepublishing
Twitter:
https://twitter.com/crystallakepub

I hope you enjoyed this title. If so, I would be grateful if you could leave a review on your blog or any of the other websites and outlets open to book reviews. Reviews are like gold to writers and publishers, since word-of-mouth is and will always be the best way to market a great book. And remember to keep an eye out for more of our books.

Crystal Lake Publishing also publishes novels, short story collections, poetry collections, non-fiction books on writing, and novellas. If you're a big fan of non-fiction books related to the Dark Fiction genre (or whichever genre you write in), then be sure to pick up *Horror 101: The Way Forward*.

THANK YOU FOR PURCHASING THIS BOOK

www.ingramcontent.com/pod-product-compliance
Lightning Source LLC
Chambersburg PA
CBHW070455120726
47910CB00003B/1049